DANCING MADLY

Dancing Madly

Short Stories

by

BETH MEAD

BOOKS

Adelaide Books
New York / Lisbon
2019

DANCING MADLY
Short Stories
By Beth Mead

Copyright © by Beth Mead
Cover design © 2019 Adelaide Books

Published by Adelaide Books, New York / Lisbon
adelaidebooks.org

Editor-in-Chief
Stevan V. Nikolic

For any information, please address Adelaide Books
at info@adelaidebooks.org
or write to:
Adelaide Books
244 Fifth Ave. Suite D27
New York, NY, 10001

ISBN-10: 1-950437-77-9
ISBN-13: 978-1-950437-77-1

Printed in the United States of America

For my parents, Marianne and Larry Lemp,
for showing me how to be good and kind, how to continue on
when life keeps throwing things in your way.

Contents

Sketching Venice

In fourth grade, Janie would chase the boys, back them into corners. Kiss their pale cheeks. From across the playground I'd watch, flushed and trying to laugh, afraid to breathe.

At thirteen, faces dewy, hair like glass, we dreamed of running away. Janie said we'd go to Venice. She spoke of gondolas and canals and serenades. I filled notebooks with sketches of our trip, of us.

In high school, boys surrounded Janie. Later, our legs tucked under us on her bed, we'd laugh about them. How weak they were. How easy to control, with a smile, with a touch. Then senior year, Janie started seeing Chuck. He was different, she whispered to me. Her first time. I put away my drawings of Venice. She'd talk for hours about Chuck's rough hands, the way they felt on her skin. I watched her mouth as she spoke.

When they married at twenty, I wore ice-pink lace. Janie said "I do" with such force I couldn't stop shaking. At the reception, she hugged me so close I felt like part of her skin.

The night Chuck hit too hard, I held her, brought her cool cloths. I pressed my lips against her forehead, her cheek. Her mouth. Again and again. Her hair smelled of ripe tangerines.

After that night she stopped calling. Thirty-eight years of nothing. Then I saw it, the announcement about Chuck's funeral. I didn't go. I couldn't. But three months passed, long enough, I thought, and now it was time.

I knock on the door.

Let's go to Venice, I'll say. *Let's finally go.*

No answer. I knock harder.

Yes, she'll say. And *I've missed you* and *I've always loved you so.*

She opens the door.

"Janie," I say, the name like heat on my tongue.

"Yes?"

Her skin is dull now, her hair almost white. "Janie, it's me."

Janie squints, colorless eyes trying to focus on my face.

"It's Olivia."

She steps back, closes the door.

I knock again.

Her voice, wavering, old, calls out to me: "Go home, Olivia. You need to go home."

I keep knocking. I say her name over and over. I want to kick down the door. To shake her until she weeps. So many years spent waiting to be hers again. Too many years.

Nothing.

I reach into my purse, pull out a black marker. Draw on the clean white door of her home, the home she'd shared with someone else, someone who wasn't me, could never be me. I draw a gondola carrying two silhouettes, dark shapes so close together they seem like one body.

I will stand here too long, staring at the door, shaking. I'll feel the weight of my legs, the ache behind my eyes. But then I will turn away, walk to my car, start the engine. Go home.

At thirteen, Janie would always say, "We can do anything, Olivia." I'd laugh, covering my mouth with my hand. "We own the world," she'd say. "It's waiting for us."

The Former
Mrs. Jonathan Rothdale

This is fine. This all will be fine. Perhaps now I'll stand, arms open, on a rainy Paris day, thinking of things that are not you. You never wanted to see Paris, I know. You only said that to make me want you.

Now I think I'll take a class, a figure-drawing class. Spend hours studying bodies at arm's reach, pencil their curves and lines, touch them in a way you never touched me. You told me I couldn't draw. I know, I'm no artist, I realize that.

I feel fine. Like the fine in fine wine. Or the fine of fine china, see-through fragile, yet solid enough to hold something within it. When you held me, it was after I had sucked you dry, before you slept heavily in dreams of others. I look at a woman on the sidewalk now, and I see her like you must have—how her hip shapes the skirt, how the skirt slips between her legs.

I think now I will change my name. Not just my last name, that name that is you, but my first name. I'll be Scarlet, I think. Or maybe Violet. I know I will be a color. When you gave me your name, I wrapped myself inside it like an egg in tissue paper. I drew the curve of the R for hours.

Worse Than Wanting

Natalie decided she wasn't going to her mother's wake. She'd go to the funeral tomorrow, but she would not stand around for hours today, greet people, smile sadly, thank distant relatives for coming. She would not look inside the casket. Morbid, she thought. Wakes were just morbid. No point in them. So she wasn't going. Besides, she'd looked at her mother's face plenty over the last four years, visiting every other day, doing her grocery shopping every weekend, writing out her bills, cleaning her bathroom, listening to her list each ache in each section of her body, from the arthritis in her legs to the ringing in her ears. Natalie did all the things a grown daughter should do while basically waiting for her mother's life to end. She'd done enough. She was done.

Montgomery, Natalie's husband, didn't understand. "You have to be at the wake," he said. "You're her only child. Her husband's gone. It's your job."

No, thought Natalie. My job was arranging the wake and the funeral, making the phone calls to every relative, every person her mother had known in her eighty-three years who might still be around. My job was finding Mom in her musty apartment, in her recliner, feet up, TV on, too still to be asleep.

"I'm not going," Natalie said again, grabbing her purse, heading toward the garage.

"Well, I am," he said.

"Fine, have fun."

"Christ, Nat, it's not about fun. You do it because you have to do it."

But I don't want to, Natalie thought. I'm tired of doing things I don't want to do. "See you tonight." She got in her car, backed out, not knowing where she was going, only where she would not go.

Natalie and Montgomery never said the word *divorce* out loud, at least not to each other, but the possibility hung in the air around them like humidity, thick, suffocating. It clouded the words they actually did say, weighed down the simplest phrase. When someone knocked at the door, his "Can you get that?" dragged through the space between them and reached her as *Get off your lazy butt and do something besides read your magazines.* Her "What time will you be home tonight?" became *If we loved each other like we're supposed to, you'd want to leave work as soon as you could.* When Natalie quit law school and accepted an entry-level job at the art museum, she knew he thought she was giving up. But it wasn't that. She wanted to steer things in a different direction, see if it helped, if life could feel better than this. She wanted to spend her days surrounded by art, not lawyers. She wanted anything besides what she already had. She tried to explain that to her mother once, the only time in the past year she'd attempted to really talk with her. She was hard to talk to, starting to forget things, never making much sense. "Oh, no," she'd said, patting Natalie's knee with a papery hand, "there's nothing worse than wanting, dear. Don't you see?" Natalie didn't answer, just helped her mother get into bed, turned out the light, locked the front door on her way out.

After two hours of aimless driving, then an hour of walking around a shopping mall, Natalie sat down at a table in the food court. This was childish, she knew. She was acting like a teenager skipping school. Natalie sighed. She should go to the wake. She could picture Montgomery in his black pants and black tie, shaking hands, nodding, making excuses for her. Probably telling people she was too distraught, couldn't get out of bed, something embarrassing. Fine, she thought. I'll go to the damn wake. But first she ordered a salad with strawberries and sunflower seeds. Then she went into a department store and charged a dark blue dress and navy pudgy-heeled pumps, not exactly stylish, but at least not black.

When she got to the funeral home, Montgomery was still there.

"Hey," she said. "Sorry."

"Nat, you made it." He kissed her cheek the way he usually did, his lips pushed forward into an exaggerated pucker, as if to keep the kiss as far away from him as possible.

"How's it been?" Natalie looked around the almost-empty room. The air was damp, cool, and smelled vaguely of mold. Probably the carpet, Natalie thought, staring at it beneath her new shoes, the worn pattern a blur of deep red, black, and gold.

"Okay. A pretty steady stream of people. Things are winding down now."

"Sorry," she said again.

"It's fine, Nat. People seemed to understand. Nobody's upset at you."

"Right."

"Really. Everybody knows how much you did for her." He yawned. "Long day. Oh, and your Uncle Jerry kept calling me Monty again. What a jerk."

When Natalie had first met Montgomery at a college party, he'd introduced himself for about five minutes straight. "I'm Montgomery Stevens," he'd said. "Montgomery. Not Monty.

Never call me Monty. Monty's a game show host. I'm no game show host."

"So what are you, exactly?" Natalie had asked.

"The man with the beer," he'd said, handing her a cold bottle.

She laughed and took a drink. "Okay, Montgomery. Maybe I can think up a nickname for you, one you like."

But during the two years they dated and their nine years of marriage, she'd never called him anything but Montgomery. It suited him. Or maybe she hadn't tried hard enough to figure him out, not really. They decided to get married when she found out she was pregnant, and by the time she miscarried, they had reserved the hall and ordered the invitations. She'd bought the dress. There didn't seem to be a reason to call things off. So they didn't. They just did what it seemed like they were supposed to do.

"You can head home, you know," Natalie said. "You've been here all day."

"It's almost over now." Montgomery looked at his watch. "I'll wait till you're ready to go."

"So who's left to talk to?" Natalie surveyed the room, recognized the priest who had visited her mom weekly, brought her a host, blessed her.

"Don't know who that is," Montgomery said, nudging his head toward a twenty-something girl entering the room.

"Me either." The girl was tall, delicate, wearing a slim black dress. She walked straight to the casket and kneeled down on the pad in front of it. Then she started sobbing. "Good grief," said Natalie. "Who the hell *is* she?"

"Go ask her. Or I will, if you want." Montgomery smoothed his tie.

"Thanks, but I can handle it."

"Really," he said. "I don't mind."

Natalie sighed and walked over to the casket, keeping her eyes on the girl. "Hi," she whispered, resting a hand on the girl's shaking back. "I'm Natalie, Augustine's daughter."

"Oh," she said, "Natalie." She stood up, brushed her fingers across her cheeks, then offered a hand. "I've heard so much about you."

Natalie shook her damp hand. "You have?"

"Augustine talked about you a lot. You and Montgomery. I hope things are going okay for you two."

"What? I'm sorry, what was your name?" Natalie glanced over at Montgomery. He was talking to the priest. "Can we, maybe, let's go sit down and talk."

The girl glanced down at the casket one last time, crossed herself, then followed Natalie to the bench near the wall. "I'm Jessica," she said. "David's girlfriend."

"David?"

"David Howard. You know, his dad is, was, Augustine's landlord." The girl looked confused, as if this should all be obvious to Natalie.

"Oh. His dad was the landlord. Okay." She wanted to yell, *But why are you crying?*

"I visited your mom with David and Mark whenever I could. She was fascinating."

"Mark?" she said. *Fascinating?* "You visited her? Well. That was nice of you. Thoughtful."

"She told us all her stories, and she would talk about you and Montgomery. And she'd listen to us go on about our troubles—you know, us wanting to get married, my parents saying I'm too young." She pulled a tissue from her purse and blew her nose. "She really listened, you know? Well," she laughed, "of course you know. She's your mom."

"Of course." Natalie felt like her head was being filled with helium, like it might take off at any moment. "So you visited her often?"

"About once a week, I guess. Mark, he's David's best friend. He would stop by to see if she needed anything, you know, he helped out the tenants, did plumbing, stuff like that. So David and I would go, too. Just to talk, have coffee with her." Jessica started crying again, hard, shoulders shaking. "I'm sorry," she said.

"No, it's okay. I just—I'm surprised Mom never mentioned you." Natalie dug a tissue out of her purse and handed it to Jessica. "You obviously meant a lot to her."

"Oh, I know the boys did. She loved when David and Mark stopped by. She just glowed. They'd flirt with her, and she'd flirt right back."

She'd flirt?

"That's why, oh." More hard crying. "That's why this is so terrible. She always said she wanted us to be at her funeral. She said she liked knowing that when her time came, we'd be there. But David and Mark are in London this week. Mark's sister's spending the semester there, and she's in a play tonight, and they went to see her. I wanted to go too, but now I'm so glad I didn't." Jessica blew her nose again. "I called David today. They're just sick about missing this. They really wanted to be here for her."

Natalie was at a loss. This woman Jessica was talking about sounded nothing like the mother she'd been taking care of. How had they never crossed paths? Did her mother arrange for them to visit when Natalie wasn't there, to make Natalie feel like she was all her mother had? She had no idea what to say to this girl. She looked around for Montgomery, waved him over. "That's my husband," she said. "Here he comes."

"Nice to meet you, Montgomery." She stood up and shook his hand. "I'm Jessica."

Montgomery smiled. "Jessica."

"Jessica and her fiancé used to visit Mom," said Natalie.

"Oh, he wasn't my fiancé. Not officially. Your mom was helping us through all that." Jessica turned to Montgomery. "And she told us about the trouble you've had, you know, trying to conceive. I'm sorry, I know that's personal, but it's just, I feel like I know you, and I'm sorry you've been having a rough time."

Montgomery looked at Natalie, who shrugged back at him with wide eyes. He cleared his throat. "Well, thanks, Jessica, but we actually decided a while back we weren't going to have children."

"Oh. I'm sorry. I thought, well, Augustine said there had been miscarriages, and she always talked about wanting grandchildren. She said we were the next best thing, though. She really treated us like family."

Natalie rubbed her hand across her forehead, closed her eyes. "Well. Jessica. I did have two miscarriages, but that was a long time ago." She looked at her husband. "We stopped trying, decided we'd be fine on our own. That's what you said, right, Montgomery?"

He looked at her, unblinking. Natalie heard the words in his silence: *We're not fine.*

Jessica's face was pink, her eyes wet. "I feel terrible. I didn't mean to interfere, really. I just, well, I love your mom. I wanted to be here since the boys can't. I don't want to intrude. I'm going to go."

"No," Montgomery said. "Don't be silly. I'm sure Augustine would want you to be here."

"I almost forgot," Jessica said, pulling some folded papers out of her purse. "I wanted to give you this. It's her writing, her life story she was working on."

"She was writing her life story?" asked Montgomery.

"Yes, you know, David always told her she should write down all the stories she told us, about all the contests she won, her drawings, and her childhood, all that. She gave me a page or two each time we'd visit, and I typed them up." She handed them to Natalie. "So, here. This copy's for you."

"Excuse me," said Natalie. She walked out of the room, went into the hallway, leaned against the wall. She tucked the pages into her purse without looking at them. This was insane, she thought. Why didn't Mom tell her about these people, about her writing? It was like her mother had an entire life separate from Natalie, a life that was much more interesting than the one they had together. And the worst part was that Natalie felt jealous, not just of Jessica for being so close to her mother, but jealous of Mom, too, for being something more than Natalie could see. So Mom had given Jessica advice on her relationship. And all she could do for Natalie was tell her not to want anything. Well, Mom obviously wanted more than she had. She wanted grandchildren, she wanted to flirt with young men, she wanted a girl to type up her life story. But all she ever told Natalie she wanted was her weekly shopping list, coffee, bananas, milk, bagels, cream cheese, the same things every week.

Natalie hated how angry she felt, how cold. This feeling, this lack of feeling, was nothing like mourning. She felt disconnected from the fact that her mother had died. The woman who died was far from the mother Natalie wanted to remember. When Natalie was young, her mother was round and soft and safe. She was just Mom, with wispy curls and pale peach lipstick, always drawing and coloring with Natalie. Mom didn't hug, didn't gush, but Natalie never felt unloved. By high school, Natalie was too worried about herself, her boyfriends, her hair, to notice her mother much—she was just there, a given. As soon as she could, Natalie moved out, found a life of her own. She rarely visited until years later, when her mother started getting sick, when her mind started to go. Mom had faded away, at least Natalie's idea of who Mom used to be. All that was left for Natalie was guilt—guilt for leaving too soon, guilt for coming back too late. And another kind of guilt, something she couldn't say out loud: As much as Natalie had wanted to be pregnant, to have a baby, she knew she never would have been happy as a mother.

"Hey, Nat." Montgomery came out into the hall, touched Natalie's shoulder. "You okay?"

"Sure." She looked at him, tried to smile. "What the hell was that, huh?"

"No kidding."

"Is she still in there?"

"Yep. Kneeling and praying and crying again. Cute, but kind of a basket case, that one." He slid a bit of Natalie's hair behind her ear.

"Guess so." His touch felt familiar and foreign at the same time. She folded her hand over his, squeezed. Maybe Natalie didn't know what she wanted, not at all. "Sorry Mom was talking to strangers about us."

"Natalie. She's gone now. It doesn't matter."

"Right." She tried to hear what his words really meant. She couldn't tell.

"Let's go home," he said. "We've still got the funeral to-morrow to get through."

"Oh boy." Natalie kept her hand in his as they walked out to the parking lot. "My car's right here," she said.

"I'll see you at home." Montgomery started to walk away, then turned back to her. "Hey, Nat," he said.

"What?"

"Are we happy?" He smiled when he said it, but it was the kind of smile that hurt, that bent a face right in half.

"No," she said, smiling too.

"No, I guess not."

"So what now?" Natalie took out her keys, fiddled with them, waited for him to answer.

"I don't know."

She leaned back against her car. "What do you want, Montgomery?"

He moved closer to her, rested his hands on her hips. "Well," he said, "how about a beer?"

She laughed. "If you're buying."

He pressed his lips against her forehead. "Follow my car. We'll find a dive around here somewhere."

"Okay," she said.

Montgomery opened the door for her. Natalie climbed inside and rested her head against the steering wheel. She watched her husband as he walked to his car. Tonight, she thought, at least for tonight, she didn't want anything but this.

Pouring

The morning our roof nearly fell in, you drilled holes in the ceiling to release pressure, placed buckets to catch the streams. I pushed towels into corners, watched you work. Remembered why I came back to you. For days we woke to air that reeked of dampness and rot. We paced until the work was done by men whose boots left marks. I won't leave again. I'll remember that morning, how we ran to see water pour from the kitchen ceiling, down the hanging lamp, fill the blue ceramic bowl, spill past its edges. How at first we could only stand there, stunned, as it soaked across the island onto the floor. You said it looked like a waterfall.

Things that Break Us Right Open

You tear apart an orange, set the pulpy pieces on your tongue, and the smell is like being seven years old in that sun-splattered kitchen, your mom peeling off the rind for you and laying out slices on a napkin, and you'd suck out the juice and give her big wet smiles. Mom was tuna on crackers, sitcoms, red-tag-sale dresses. She'd look at you like you were everything that mattered.

You drive to work and something about the road, the way it rattles your car, makes you want to take the wrong exit, to go someplace else that's smoother and better and not-here. Your fingertips still smell like orange. If you weren't in the left lane, maybe, and there weren't so many cars around you, blocking you from getting there, you'd exit right now.

At the office, the girl with the wax-doll face calls you *sir* and looks down at her feet when you speak. You wish she'd look up, because you like to collect eyes, memories of eyes, hold them loosely in your pocket like rainy-day change. Your father's eyes were doughy, a peanut-shell beige. Soft and blank. You rub your thumb across the memory of them and feel like his boy again, muddy, pouting. Your ex-wife's eyes were milky blue. Your first girlfriend had eyes like candle flame, slick with light.

You drive home. The stillness feels familiar but wrong. You slide off your shoes, turn on the TV, turn off the TV. You tear apart an orange.

The Train

People are just stupid, Reg thought. Stupid dumb stupidheads.

The person most recently annoying Reg, Green-Hooded Sweatshirt Boy, was driving the car in front of him, playing drums on his steering wheel, bobbing his green-hooded head up and down. He could feel the bass from the boy's radio, tinny and thumping. Reg moved to the left lane, passed Sweatshirt Boy's car, then pulled right back in front of it. Then, like Reg knew he would, the boy got into the left lane and sped past him. He probably gave Reg a nasty look as he drove by, but Reg didn't turn to see it. Stupidhead kid.

Reg loosened his grip on the steering wheel. He hadn't realized how tightly he'd been squeezing it, how white and shiny his knuckles were. He didn't even want to be here, in this cold car that would never heat up, headed for the damn train station. He was only here because of his breathing, the way it would stop sometimes when he slept, wake him up, cause him to gasp and sit up and wipe the sweat from his forehead. Going up stairs, too, his legs heavy with each step, leaning into the handrail, his breath would leave him. He'd have to stop midway, fill his lungs, bend his stiff knees a few times, before he could continue.

After a few months of this he went to a doctor about it, paid a lousy twenty-dollar co-pay for some pinched-up woman to say, in a tight little voice, "Lose fifty pounds." At least she'd said it without pity. Back when he still worked at the office, before he got the laptop set-up, the work-at-home sweet deal, the guys would talk about him, about his weight, like he was some toy for them to play with. They'd say he looked good, like a man who knew how to live, then pat his soft back. Reg never said anything back to them, just shook his head, shrugged.

"Get out more," Dr. Pinch-face had said to him, writing in the chart, not looking at him as she spoke. "Do something different, something you wouldn't normally do. To get yourself started."

Reg stared at Pinchy's eyebrows, the way they scrunched together when she talked.

"Maybe try rollerblading," she said. "There's a good path at Sunset Park."

Reg coughed into his fist, thinking, rollerblading? What, was she crazy? Some crazy insane crazy-person? He watched her walk out the door with a little swing of her pinched-up hips. Reg pictured himself trying to balance on two thin rows of colored wheels, and he decided Pinchy was making fun of him. Well. He'd show her what he could do.

So Reg decided to do a bunch of things he didn't like all at once. Get it over with faster. A train ride was just what he needed: lots of annoying people to have to look at, deal with; seats too small for him to fit into comfortably; and leaving his city, well, just leaving his house was enough, really, enough to make him all itchy. He'd gotten used to the comfort of staying home, ordering in food, sending out work by email, never having to stray too far, do too much. But he had to admit it wasn't working for him anymore, not when he couldn't sleep, when each night was a struggle to get through. A train ride would get him started, like Dr. Pinch-face said. Then he could go back to her and say, See, look what I did, I'm not some stupidhead lazy jerk.

Reg pulled into the commuter lot and waited for his car to chug to a stop. People were bundled up, scurrying toward the station. He cracked open the car door and felt the air around him get even colder. With a lurch he swung his body sideways, used his hand to help unwedge one bulky leg and get it down to the asphalt. Reg took a deep breath then heaved his body upward, making sure his feet were firmly planted, balanced, before he looked up and saw a woman passing by. She glanced away from Reg as soon as he looked up, and Reg knew what she was thinking: Big clumsy oaf, can't even get out of a car like a normal person. Looks ready to pass out, that's what she thought, while she was trying so hard not to stare. Forget her, he thought, Miss Long and Lean, all draped in black, black hat, black hair, black coat, black boots. Black black black blah blah blah. She probably dressed all in black every single day, thought it made her look dramatic. Who cared what she thought.

Reg lifted his jacket's stiff yellow collar and ducked his head, chin pressed to chest, as if that would block the chilled wind, and made his way to the station. As the train pulled in with its metal scrape of brakes straining against the tracks, the rain began. Icy rain, so cold it felt hot when it hit skin. Blast it all, Reg thought. Picked quite a day for this train ride of mine. After a wait that was way too long, and way too cold, he grabbed the small metal handrail and hoisted himself forward to board the train.

A white-haired, white-faced, milky-white man checked his ticket and pointed Reg down the aisle. Reg turned sideways and scooted his legs along the narrow aisle, feeling eyes on him, feeling his face prickle from the stares. He lowered himself into a seat by a window, a seat with curved-up edges that dug into the bottoms of his thighs. He wiped the sweat from above his lip, across his forehead. Leaned forward, his hands on his knees. Sat back again. Wondered what the hell he was doing here. The inside of the train was not at all like he'd imagined it would be. He should've known better. He'd pictured—what? An old-fashioned locomotive, with ornate dining cars, large sleeping areas. Plush red, he'd thought, with gold trim. But this train was dull, too much metal, smelled of window cleanser. Everything was industrial gray or dirtied-up blue. Reg looked out the window. The rain had quickened, become denser, louder. Bits of ice hit with a tink-tink against the glass. He wondered if train travel was safe in this kind of rain, if the tracks would get slick, if he would hydroplane to his death. He laughed at himself, shook his head.

As the announcements began over the speakers, with every few words too scratchy to be heard, a young man hurried along the aisle. Don't sit by me, Reg thought. Skinny thing, this guy was, skinny like a stick, tall and wiry and girly, with his cheekbones and little pointy nose. Too pretty for a guy, he thought, and probably all prissy, wouldn't talk to someone like me if I paid him. Luckily StickMan sat in the row in front of Reg, so Reg had some room to breathe, didn't have to wedge himself against the window to stay in his own seat. He stretched his legs wide apart, rested his head back. Then he started feeling conspicuous and sat back up straight again. He looked at the old guy reading the newspaper across the aisle from him, probably retired, probably just riding the train for no reason like me, Reg thought, just bought a round-trip ticket for something to do. Maybe he's trying to get away from his whiny old wife for a while. Retired Guy sneezed, and Reg was surprised StickMan didn't say "Bless you" in some girly voice. Nobody blessed Retired Guy. He just blew his nose in a handkerchief, the white linen kind, which the wife probably ironed for him. He wore a jean jacket, of all things, and blue jeans, but he was wearing shiny brown shoes—probably the shoes he used to wear to work every day until he retired, took the early option package, thinking he and the wife could fall in love again, travel, he'd stop hating her so much. But instead he puts on those shoes and comes here to ride the train and read the paper.

The train felt alive beneath Reg's feet, but it hadn't started moving forward yet. Sleet was hitting the windows and roof hard now. Stupid storm, Reg thought. He started rubbing his fingers, feeling them clench up. Let's get moving, he thought. A little girl a few rows up started crying, saying Mommy-Mommy-Mommy a lot, pulling on her mother's coat sleeve. She had that little-girl hair, fuzzy and airy and uncombed, and her jacket was halfway off her shoulders. Just a mess, Reg thought, that girl's scared and a mess, and that mother should do something. Reg didn't even like kids, but he wished that mother would comb the girl's hair, button up her coat. Instead the mother was shushing her, pink-faced, embarrassed. Reg looked at the mother and wanted to shake her, to tell her to relax and stop worrying about what other people were thinking. The kid's just scared. Reg rubbed his hands over his knees and looked out the window.

The speaker was scratching out announcements again. Something about clearing the tracks, safety precautions. People were starting to get up and leave, so Reg pulled himself to his feet. Just great, he thought, there really was a problem. He almost asked Retired Guy if he'd heard what exactly was going on, but the words didn't come out in time, so he just followed down the aisle behind him.

The milky-white ticket man was standing in front near the steps, telling people not to worry, being vague. Everyone was too close together in the aisle, Reg thought. Too much shuffling forward, moving too fast. Reg grabbed the metal rail at the doors and lowered himself from the train. As he stepped down, his foot slid on the slick pavement. He felt his hand fall from the rail and his elbow smack against the metal step. His legs flew forward, feet in the air, and Reg landed hard on his tailbone. He tried to get up quickly but slid back down, flat on his back.

Stop, he thought. Stop moving.

He rested his head back against the ground and looked up into the falling rain. The noise of people gathering around him mixed with the sound of sleet. He didn't move, just thought about how wet and cold he felt, and how ridiculous he must look, like when he was in fourth grade and the Breiser brothers pushed him down at recess, the two of them with their big noses and curly hair, like a couple of clowns. Reg wasn't even fat then, no reason to get picked on except that he just didn't talk much, not much to say to the dumb-asses at school anyway, but that day the Breiser brothers wouldn't let up. Reg couldn't remember why, but they kept poking him with a baseball bat, poking and pushing him, and then Jack or Joe, he didn't know which, shoved the damn bat down the front of Reg's pants, hurt like hell, then pushed him flat on his back and ran off. He remembered laying there, looking at the sky, not moving, hardly breathing, noticing everything—muffled stomps of feet on the playground, squeaking laughter around him, and high above him, the way the clouds were scratched across the sky, thready and weightless. But now, looking up into the rain, Reg could only see StickMan's face hovering over him.

"Here, grab my hand. I'll help you up." StickMan's voice wasn't girly at all, Reg thought. Not what he'd expected.

Reg sat up slowly on his own. He rolled over to his side, then braced both hands on one knee and pushed himself up to a stand. His elbow and his ass hurt like hell. He didn't look at StickMan, not at anyone, just walked through the rain to the overhang where the rest of the passengers were standing, waiting.

If this isn't a sign, Reg thought, I don't know what is. Just go home. Who cares what Dr. Pinch-face says. I'll be fine. Silly idea, anyway. Train ride. What the hell was I thinking.

Reg stood there for a while, watched the rain slow, soften. He saw the ticket man move back to the train steps, wave everyone over. He watched people board the train, the messy little girl and her mother, Retired Guy, Miss Long and Lean. StickMan was still standing by Reg, taking pity on the poor fat guy who fell, he guessed.

"Ready?" StickMan said to Reg.

It would be so easy to turn around and leave, Reg thought. Just turn and go. He knew how to make life easy. It didn't have to be hard.

StickMan motioned for Reg to follow him, then walked toward the train. Reg took a step and felt the ache in his back, down through his legs. He thought about the Breiser brothers, and watched StickMan walking away, and he started to remember something else about that day at school, something he'd forgotten. That silly little girl from his fourth-grade class, what was her name? Ella. Yes. She'd walked over to him while he was laying there like some idiot on the playground, the baseball bat still sticking out of his pants, and she'd sat down right there next to him. He'd yanked out the bat, thrown it aside, but he didn't talk, didn't look at her. What did she say? Something like, "Look, Chiclets—take some if you want." Her hand looked so tiny, so delicate, holding out that flat little box. And then she whispered, "Chew slow and the teacher can't tell." Reg remembered that he took some, a handful of the tiny colored plasticky gum, and he got up and walked over to the school building. He stood against the brick wall, and it felt cool and comforting, and he chewed that gum all at once, all the tangy flavors mixing together, and it tasted sweet and sticky. He leaned against that wall and chewed his Chiclets and waited for recess to end. Reg didn't remember saying thanks to the girl, to Ella, he was sure he didn't. But it was one of those small moments, a good moment. Funny he'd forgotten about that.

Reg started walking toward the ticket man, one hand on his stinging elbow, and got back on the train. He made his way to his seat by the window, sat down slowly. Finally, the train lurched forward, started its heavy pull from the station. Thick smoke, sooty gray, swelled against the window before disappearing into the light mist of rain. The seats rattled with the train's jerking, churning motion.

StickMan turned around to look at him. "You okay?" he asked Reg.

Reg noticed his fingers, how tightly he was gripping his knees. He stretched his hands open, rubbed his knuckles.

"You know," said StickMan, "the ride gets smoother as you go."

Reg cleared his throat. "Thanks," he said.

"Sure." StickMan turned back around.

The fuzzy-haired girl was leaning against her mother's arm now, and Reg thought maybe it was seeing her that made him remember Ella and her Chiclets, or maybe it was falling on the ground so hard. Whatever it was, he hadn't thought about that in ages, and the memory hit him like a wind.

Daylight Savings

Matt was right. I should've remembered to change the alarm clock. Spring forward, easy as that. Like he said, he could've lost his job, being an hour late. Then where would we be? Maybe he looked like he was going to hit me, but he didn't.

His heart was in the right place, Mama would say. To explain away anything Matt did. Like it was about location, his heart, being where it should be. *He meant well.* I nod like I agree. Mama was just relieved I'd found a husband, had a son. Everything after that didn't matter so much to her. *When you're a wife and a mother, it all makes sense,* she'd say. Like a book had been closed. No point in reading it again, hoping for a different ending.

But on good days when Timmy takes a nap after lunch, I go out on the front porch, close the door behind me. Think about how I'd pack just a few things, wear a white summer dress. I stand there on the porch alone, and it's like I'm riding in a fancy car with the top down. Letting the sun drench my skin.

All is Well

11:00 and all is well. I sit on the living room floor with my daughter, our legs tucked under us, and we sip quick-shop wine from our plastic cups. We are waiting for midnight, for the shiny new year with its promise to wipe away the messiness of our past. My daughter Sarah is too young for wine, only sixteen, but I tell her tonight it's okay. Saying this feels like I'm giving chocolate milk to a baby; a guilty pleasure done entirely for myself. Somewhere beneath Sarah's too-made-up eyes, her short-cropped hair, I can see the pale blonde curls I formed around her pouting face each morning when she was my Shirley Temple, my little girl. She's still my little girl. And tonight she is hurting and I will rock her to sleep.

"Mom, this really tastes awful, you know," Sarah says, smiling sideways at me.

"I know, bug." I take another sip. Sarah is stuck with me for New Year's Eve because she broke up with Craig last week. Since then she has kept herself hidden from me even more than usual. She walks quietly, slowly, without picking up her feet. I assume Craig was her first boyfriend, her first love, although I'm not privy to the details of her life these days. All I know is she asked to stay home with me tonight in a mumbling sort of way that made me respond calmly, off-handedly,

"Sure." It wasn't until Sarah left the room that I staggered and had to lean against the wall to catch my breath. It used to be unspoken, simply understood that we would spend holidays like this together. But now she is a teenager with a life outside of me. I'll take whatever I can get.

Sarah makes a dramatic gagging sound. She leans forward to set her cup on the coffee table and picks up the remote.

I don't want the television on. I want her to talk to me and tell me about her life, about herself, this self she has now that I'm not allowed to touch. "Let's wait until it's closer to midnight," I say lightly.

"Whatever." Sarah stands and carries her cup to the kitchen.

I climb up onto the couch, my knees cracking loudly. I can't quite accept that I have become this person, this mother, with dimpled thighs and lines around my lips and an inability to stomach the music my daughter plays behind the closed door of her room. When I was pregnant with Sarah, all of twenty-two and strangely fearless, I couldn't picture myself growing older. Or at least I thought by now I would be wise and elegant and admired by my children. I bragged with confidence to Phil, my now-ex-husband, even while I was in labor.

"This isn't so bad," I had told Phil for the third time in as many contractions. "I can do this again. We can have lots of babies." I kept my eyes closed as I spoke to him.

"We'll see," he said, spooning out crushed ice from a plastic cup, feeding me like a baby bird. "Let's get through this one first, okay?"

"I want a big family," I said through clenched teeth, bracing myself for the heated, ripping pain beginning again in my lower back. Phil had proposed immediately when he found out I was pregnant, which I thought was romantic and made everything okay. But I could tell part of him resented me. He felt he was missing out on something; he didn't have to say it. I heard it in his voice when he spoke to me, heavy and cold, like a clammy hand.

"Amanda," Phil had said quietly once I was resting again. "I have a big family, you know. It isn't that great." He fed me another spoonful of ice chips.

"We can get a new house for the second or third baby," I said, crunching loudly.

"It's hard to have a bunch of brothers and sisters. Too much noise, too much competition. Never enough hot water." Phil had moved to the rocking chair in the corner. He yawned and rocked, yawned and rocked.

"I can handle having a big family," I said into my cup of ice. "And the kids'll be stronger for it. You'll see. They'll adore us."

But I never went on to have children, just a child. It was just me and Sarah. The icy wall between Phil and me only grew thicker, and before long he found someone else to be romantic with. We divorced when Sarah was two, when most of my friends were getting engaged. For months I felt numb as I moved through each day. I took all the vacation time my secretarial job allowed, kept Sarah home from nursery school, and lived on chocolate ice cream and sausage pizza. I made weekly late-night trips to the 24-hour drugstore to buy candy bars and fashion magazines, feeling both guilty and hopeful. While Sarah slept, I would curl up on the couch and read articles like "Ten Tips to Trimmer Hips," leaving chocolate-brown thumbprints on the glossy pages.

After a while I was able to convince myself that divorce was better than the alternatives, being blindly cheated on or slowly forgotten, and I decided to embrace my life alone with Sarah. When she started first grade, we would talk every morning over cheesy scrambled eggs; I helped her with homework, kissed her forehead every night before bed. It felt like enough.

There was a time, about five years ago now, when I thought I might allow a man to enter our little world. He was Bob, sweet, simple Bob, who made me pancakes and brought Sarah books on reptiles, her obsession at the time. He found a small piece of me that still ached for a man's hand on my knee. But somehow I wasn't willing, couldn't find enough energy, to start life all over like that. Sarah and I were fine on our own. Life felt easier that way. So I stopped answering the phone. I waited to feel lonely, but instead I felt relief. Eventually, the phone didn't ring anymore. And that was that.

11:22 and all is well. I have given in to watching television since my gentle nudging is not getting Sarah to talk. But she is sitting next to me on the couch, and I can tell she likes the band playing noisily on TV. I risk smoothing down her hair, resting my hand on her shoulder for a second. She offers me a grin. Then her phone rings and I lose her again.

"Hello," Sarah says, walking into the kitchen.

I decide it's too late for a phone call, even if it is New Year's Eve, and I get up to tell her so. I stop at the kitchen doorway for a moment, listening to the voice I never hear, the one reserved for her friends, bubbly, energized. Happy. I turn away, about to head back to the couch, when Sarah's voice changes suddenly.

"Put Monica back on the phone, Craig," says Sarah. "I don't want to talk to you."

There is a shaky anger to her words that makes me enter the kitchen. I whisper, "What's wrong?" Sarah glares at me and goes to her room, the door shutting with a thud behind her. I follow but stop at the closed door, lean against the wall, close my eyes. I am the mother. I need to go in there. I try to hear what Sarah is saying, but instead I hear someone on TV describing the bits of Waterford crystal that cover the massive ball waiting to drop in Times Square.

Now Sarah is sticking her head out the door. "Mom, I'm going to Monica's party after all, okay?"

"No." I stand, open her door all the way and take the phone from her hand.

Sarah lunges toward me but I step back and put the phone behind my back. Sarah pauses, then casually laughs. "Monica's picking me up. I'm going to the party," she says.

"No, you're not. You're staying home with me. You're going to tell me about this Craig." I grab her hand, her fingers stubbornly limp, and pull her to the living room. I will not let my daughter slip away from me, not tonight.

My first night with Sarah, right after she was born, I expected to feel the overwhelming joy, the pure love, that my mother had promised I'd feel. Mom said she instantly felt complete when she held me for the first time. But I felt lost, entirely separate from the moist, puckered creature that had been placed across my chest. I didn't tell Phil; I barely admitted it to myself. It wasn't until six weeks later, as I started sleeping for three hours in a row instead of in twenty-minute stretches, that I began to love my baby. We were snowed in together for a week. My maternity leave was up and I should have been sitting at my receptionist desk, but the snowstorm was a good excuse to prolong my break from reality. I watched people shovel and scrape their cars from behind the window of Sarah's room; I held my baby in my arms, pressed into me, all day long. She slept with her mouth on my skin, and she would wake every so often to suck, and curl her toes, and rub her palm along the tip of her ear. I could smell her in my clothes, a tangy smell like cider and tender sweat. I touched her eyelids, swollen like little eggshells, and called her my bug in singing mommy whispers. As I nursed her, I knew she would be my purpose in life when I couldn't find one for myself. For nine months, she had been a part of my body; now I was becoming part of hers.

Of course, her body is too grown up now, too round and full for her age. It was the same for me at sixteen. I looked older than I was in a way that seemed to cry out for boys' hands and lips. I assume this woman's body is the cause of Sarah's troubles, that Craig wanted to move too fast for her. I want to tell Sarah to be careful, so careful, to wait until she knows she's ready. I can remember the pressure; I enjoyed the lingering glances, the attention, but I never wanted more than that until college, when I met Phil. Phil was achingly beautiful, and I longed for him. I gave every bit of myself to him, too easily, too often. Admiration like that can be hypnotic. I want Sarah to know that I understand how she feels, that I've been there.

11:47 and all is well. Sarah has realized I will not let her leave the couch until she starts talking, and so she is finally humoring me, telling me about Craig. Her hands are drawn up into her sweater sleeves, with only her fingertips poking through, and she picks at her dark purple nail polish as she talks.

"He sits across from me in Spanish class. We'd talk sometimes, and then he started texting me during class, with his phone under the desk. Sometimes he got caught." Sarah smiles, a private sort of smile that doesn't include me. "But it was sweet."

"And then you started going out? Dating?" I didn't even know what to call it, just knew that it wasn't called going steady anymore.

"Yeah." She sighs and starts biting her thumbnail. "He's so cute, Mom. And he really loves me. He loves me so much, and he hates it when we're apart. He likes to know where I am all the time, who I'm with. One time when I was at Monica's, he texted me a hundred and seven times."

"What? Sarah, that's not okay."

"Chill, Mom, I know. I told him that was stupid. He got mad, but after a while he calmed down." Now Sarah is playing with the high neck of her sweater, rubbing the material between her fingertips. "He really was sweet sometimes."

"He sounds too controlling." I lift her chin so I can see her face. "Is that why you broke up with him, Sarah?" I smile gently at her. "Or was he pressuring you? You know, to do too much, things you weren't ready for?"

Sarah looks at me, expressionless. The sudden coldness of her eyes stops my breath, takes away my smile. My ears start to pound as a voice on TV counts backwards from ten. Sarah's mouth turns down at the corners; her lower lip, full and soft and colored burnt orange, starts trembling. I can smell the cheap wine on the table next to me, a tart, fruity smell that hangs thickly in the air. It sickens me and I concentrate on it fully, breathing it in, so that the smell is more real than my daughter's fingers as they peel down the soft collar of her sweater, revealing her neck. The bruises are mostly deep blue, fading into yellow at the edges. I can tell the marks are the shape of fingers, of Craig's hands squeezing her neck, thick lines circling her throat like a broken necklace.

I try to speak. "Oh, bug," I say faintly. How could I think Sarah has the same simple worries I had at sixteen? This is a different world, and she lives in it, is part of it, while I just watch from behind the glass. Sarah's fingers drop to her lap and her neck is covered again. I hear a car horn, loud and insistent, and when Sarah looks to the door I realize the sound is not someone celebrating the close of the year. It is Monica, waiting to take my daughter away. My body goes numb. The TV voice is finishing the countdown as Sarah rises.

"He won't do it again, Mom. I know he won't." She opens the front door. "He loves me. I'll be okay."

The noise from the television is deafening. The door closes and I run toward it. I feel like I'm in a dream, running through a muddy trench, my feet weighted and slowing with each step. I finally reach the door, fling it open, run down the driveway. I want my baby. I want to hold her, wrap her in warm blankets, kiss her hair, sing her to sleep. But the car is gone. 12:00.

When the Rain Stops

Kayleigh whined for weeks that she wanted a haircut. Soon, I said. After I get paid. After I finish cleaning out the garage. I'm so tired. Next week, when the rain stops. Soon.

She started scratching the back of her head and behind her ears, like a puppy, while watching TV, while doing homework at the kitchen table. Stop that, I said. I could tell she was trying to get under my skin, to punish me for putting her off. I did that, I knew. Put her off. It really itches, she said. It's the cold weather, I told her, the dry heat in the house. I believed that. Stop acting like such a teenager, I said.

Of course, of course, when I finally took her to the salon, the stylist called me over. I can't cut her hair with evidence of live lice, she said, giving me that look, that combination of judgment and pity. Kayleigh's body was small, collapsed in on itself in the chair, head down, eyes closed. Her hand went up to scratch her head, stopped, and fell back to her lap.

Thank you, I said, and took Kayleigh's hand, held it as we walked out the door, as we walked to the car. I hadn't held her hand like that since she was a little girl, when she was fragile in a different way, easy to protect. When getting through each day didn't make me so tired. I started the car and then looked at her, kept looking until she looked back. Don't worry, I said. I'm going to take care of you.

Mothers

My grandmother lived in bed. Her ankles were swollen, hard to walk on, but she wasn't ill. Not really, not physically. Depression was shameful then. My grandmother's bed was in the living room of her small home, the kitchen to her left, the closet with her portable toilet to the right. Her husband died of cancer. Her youngest son shot himself in a field. She died in front of a television. As children, we climbed up next to her and listened to her stories about the teddy bears who lived in the woods in the painting above her bed. She would draw me paper dolls to cut out and dress, girls with wide eyes and curled bangs and beauty marks on their cheeks. My grandmother was an artist.

My mother sometimes worked three jobs, three shifts, to pay the bills that my father would not pay after he left, to raise the children he no longer saw. She married another man to help pay the bills, told me later how she knew on her wedding day, standing in our backyard in her powder blue dress, that she was making a terrible mistake. That man drank every day. He was accused of things that my mother prayed were not true. My mother's youngest daughter punched her in the stomach in an emergency room, stole from her, asked her how much money she'd leave behind when she dies. With husband number three, my mother got a new home away from the past, and road trip vacations, and finally retirement. She talks me off ledges and takes me to lunch, to musicals, to movies. My mother is a survivor.

I'm a terrible mother. I somehow missed that my youngest son has been depressed and suicidal since he was eleven. I somehow missed that he has been drinking and doing drugs for years. Until a policeman knocked on my door at 3am, I somehow missed that my son was sneaking out of our house, meeting up with people in the neighborhood park where I took him as a child, where I pushed him on swings and wished he'd get tired enough to nap. I took my son to counselors and doctors and clinics. I gained a hundred pounds. My husband lost three jobs. Every morning I dread getting out of bed. But some days, there is art. Some days, we survive. Some days, I hold my son close and remember how to be a mother.

Portraits

My Son at 15 in a Jail Cell

We didn't see him walk into the cell. We only saw before, as we all sat in the small room with its metal table and chairs, its cinder block walls. We saw the deep red marks on his wrists where the handcuffs had dug in. We saw his eyes, all of it in his eyes—the masked terror, the resolution to endure this, the disbelief. We felt that disbelief, looked at it from high above ourselves: what a fascinating thing, that this could really be happening. We filled out paperwork. We kept patting his back, as if that could help. We did not cry, not before, because he did not cry. We were strong because he was strong. We hugged him like it was forever, like it was an ending. We did not sob until later, when he was inside a jail cell and we were home in bed, under heavy blankets, the hum of the heater around us, keeping us warm.

My Son Onstage

The electric guitar starts while the stage is still empty. My son, a middle-schooler who is too handsome and self-assured for his years, appears stage left and saunters to the microphone stand. He is casual and cool and belts out Green Day like it's breathing. The audience cheers and claps and whispers about him to each other, *so young, so talented*. The audience doesn't see the cuts on his forearm in neat rows, doesn't hear that voice in his head telling him he is worthless. They see that swoop of hair, that charming smile. They hear him sing like a rockstar, think to themselves, *what a lucky kid. What a life he'll have.*

My Infant Son, Suddenly Gone

Ice coated the parking lot. I stepped slowly, planting my feet. I unbuckled my four-year-old and steadied him next to me. I pulled my newborn from his carseat and pressed him against my chest, his head against my neck. (Why didn't I use the carrier, keeping him buckled inside? Why did I leave the house to drive to preschool in the ice and bitter cold?) I made it inside, left my older son to color and count, to eat snacks and nap. Then I wrapped both arms around my infant son and stepped back onto the parking lot. Deliberate steps, careful. Made it to the car, reached into my coat pocket to get my keys. Then slipped. Fell hard, one hand against the side of the ice-coated car, one hand on the ice-coated ground. Aching, trying to catch my breath. And then realizing: I was not holding my baby.

I looked all around me, scrambled to get up, trying to understand what happened. I could not see my baby. I could not hear my baby. (Why couldn't I hear my baby? Why didn't he cry?) I finally got to my feet, hands against the car, sturdy. I looked down and my infant son was under the car, a blanketed bundle next to the tire. I had dropped my baby and he slid under the car. I'd slipped and my arms went out to brace myself instead of staying wrapped around my son. (How is that possible? How am I a mother?) I reached for my baby, pulled him to me, kissed his head. He was breathing, he was fine, but still he made no sound.

I got into the back seat of the car, pulled off his blanket, wet from the icy ground. I pulled a fresh blanket out of his diaper bag and wrapped him in it. I tried to breastfeed him, offering myself as comfort, as apology, but he would not latch on. He was still silent. (Why didn't I go to the emergency room? Or call his doctor?) I buckled him back into his carseat. I climbed up to the front seat and drove home. My son, my infant son who fell under a car, was sleeping when I carried him inside. I put him in his crib and sat at the kitchen table. For hours I sat there and waited to hear him wake up, hoping for him to cry, for everything to be fine. And he did, and it was. I didn't tell my husband what happened, didn't tell anyone. I just felt the shame of it, and lived with that, and still keep it inside me. I hold onto it like a warning.

Present

I do not have the answers for you. You come at me, sword and scream blazing. I will sit here in my red dress and look at your eyes until you slow. Your hand unclenches, falls to your side. I will sit here as days spin behind us like thick yarn unspooled. You want more from me. To offer this ankle, to make you a gift of this chin. I have nothing for you that you do not already own. Take your things and go. In this late-day light, splintered across your face like thrown glass, I forget all that has come before. Only this bench, that soft hill there. The redheaded girl on the swing, chains creaking. Her dirty shoes drag through the sand.

Devoured

His eyes were resting on my skin the way a fresh canker sore sits on the inside of a cheek, slightly pulsing, softly teasing that it's moments away from erupting into an ache that consumes all thought. I pretended not to notice. I picked a curl of lint from my sweater sleeve and watched it float to the carpet. I knew his type, knew exactly what a man like this would do to me. He would peel my heart with a blunt knife, slowly curling around its edges as if he were skinning an apple in one long strip. After robbing me of that layer of thin protection, he knew he could easily, at any moment he chose, sink his teeth directly into me. The misshapen, darkening core that remained would be his trophy, shelved to collect dust until it was covered and forgotten.

I sneezed.

"Gesundheit," he offered, taking the opportunity to slide into the chair next to me. "They say a doctor's waiting room is the easiest place to get sick." He posed it as a question, his eyes on my lips, waiting for me to speak.

"I guess it keeps them in business," I said. Then I looked away. I was always trying to censor myself, afraid of saying too much. Michael used to say I gave myself too freely to strangers. I couldn't help it. The hint of new love melts in my mouth, tasting of honeydew melon, thick and sweet. I'd suck every bit of flavor from it, slurping, biting, devouring, and my appetite would only grow and grow.

I suddenly decided to find the hem of my skirt terribly interesting.

"I never go to the doctor," he continued. "I mean, here I am, but it's really not something I like to do. As a rule." He leaned back against the worn upholstery, allowing his arm to drape along the armrest between us.

I glanced down at his hand. The fingers were too long, the knuckles too bony, the skin too smooth. No ring. I watched as he ran his fingertips along the edge of the armrest, slowly, deliciously. I looked up at his face and felt punctured, as if a great wind were being sucked into the pit of my stomach. Too pretty.

"How about you?" He leaned slightly toward me and lifted a piece of lint from my shoulder. "Do you frequent the good doctor?" He flashed a juicy grin.

I felt a pang when his fingers brushed against me. What was he thinking, just reaching out and touching a stranger like that? "I'm just here for a physical. For my new job. I thought I could squeeze it in on my lunch hour. I always forget how long they make you wait." Stop talking, I thought. I looked down at my watch, a gift from Michael, a piece of him that hadn't been removed from my life yet. He mostly gave me useless things, like the waterproof Boy Scout compass I kept running across in my purse. When Michael gave it to me, he said, "As long as you know which way is north, you can never get lost." Even then, I didn't believe him. To me, north is up, and I can always get lost.

I pulled my sleeve down over the watch.

"Allergies," he said. "They make me come back every year or so just to keep giving me the same prescription. Don't you hate that?" His stomach growled loudly enough for me to hear.

"Hmmm." How presumptuous, I thought, the way he kept inviting me into his personal conversation. I crossed my legs away from him and thought of Becca, the one Michael decided to love next. When I ran into them that lonely day at the museum, where Michael and I had so often spent afternoons together, I was still wearing his lousy watch. Of course he noticed, smugly looked at it hanging around my wrist without saying a word. He just scooped up Becca's hand into his. Becca put on her candle wax smile, dripping and hot. She had sun-goddess skin and pouting lips the size of my fingertips. Her hair was short and sleek, how Michael always wanted me to cut mine. I couldn't, not even for him. Like Samson, I needed my hair, needed its length, its thick net of safety and power. It didn't help me that day, of course. Open-mouthed and lost, I stared at Michael as the seconds hung in the air, strung like beads. "Good to see you," he finally said. Then he walked away with Becca, her heels clicking stony echoes off the art-lined walls. Part of me almost pitied Becca, knowing what was in store for her. He didn't really love her. He favored her, gave her selected bits of his affection, like gold stars to lick and display. The glue would dry, her glow would fade from his sight, and she would be left watching someone new click away with Michael.

I pulled back my sleeve and looked at the watch.

"What time do you have?" he asked.

"Ten to one." I sighed, knowing I'd never make it back to work on time. "I don't know why I care," I said, and then realized I had spoken out loud. "Oh. Well. I'm at the end of my two weeks' notice. I start my new job Monday. I'll be late getting back, but I guess it doesn't really matter that much. Not anymore." I glanced at him, then looked away.

"Right. What are they going to do, fire you?" He turned his whole body toward me in the chair.

I laughed and recrossed my legs toward him. "This week's been tough," I said. "No one's talking to me at work. And last night, I cried watching a sitcom because I couldn't stop seeing the characters as actors, as people with full lives, and I was just sitting on a couch, eating microwave popcorn, watching them do their job." I stopped myself. Too much too much too much.

He studied my face for a moment and then smiled. He was practically smacking his lips.

I felt like I was swirling. Other men who made me feel like this came rushing back to me. Like Stewart. Stew, I called him, feeling it fit. He was thick; he was wedged potatoes and beef. He was comfort food, until he was gone. Then Roman, like a sculpture, hard and smooth. I felt important with him. I'd hang on his arm, lean into his chest. But he looked at me and saw a messy watercolor girl—faded, no distinct edges, not quite worthy of his frame. And Curt, unemployed, dreamy. He wrote dark, needy poetry. We wrapped ourselves in his sheets and sat on his fire escape steps, watching the world pass by below us. Weeks of this, drinking coffee like it was food, watching him smoke his cigarettes. Then watching his interest fade as quickly as it came. On and on, like some mad dance, so many turns, so many men. I needed to stop spinning.

The nurse opened the door and called out his name like a bell. "Jake?"

Jake stood up, started walking toward the nurse, then looked back at me. "So, if you aren't too busy tonight, want to grab something to eat?"

I squinted up at him, looked into his eyes. I could feel him scraping out pieces of my heart with a spoon, licking the edges afterward to make sure he got every last bit. I only paused a moment. "Absolutely."

Long Lost

I found that photo today, the one with a blurred edge of thumb hiding your mouth. I'm sure you were smiling—it's there in your eyes. Like water, those eyes. I drank them over and over and over. Where are you now? Do you watch the morning bruise of sky with her hand light on your chest? Cover my eyes again. See that day of lilacs, wine staining our lips. Find me in your drawer of lost things. I wait there, my veins shining blue through the clear skin of my wrist. I wait like this.

In the Breakroom

Mary Ellen overheard Dave say to Tracy that Andrew wasn't getting the promotion, that they were going outside the company to fill it, and that Andrew was on to them, knew he was getting screwed, and so he was going to do something, something big.

Mary Ellen heard lots of things like that, things that were never said to her directly but she heard them anyway, tucked them away until they were especially useful. And she knew I'd care, because I'd slept with Andrew fourteen times, and even though Andrew and I weren't speaking anymore and wouldn't even nod at each other in the breakroom, Mary Ellen knew I'd want to hear about it. And then I'd owe her somehow, and if she ever needed to switch days off she'd look at me and twist her fuzzy brown hair around her finger in that way that means *You owe me, you know you do,* and of course I'd say yes.

So I nodded at her with serious eyes and said "Thanks!" and took off to linger around the outside of Andrew's cube. You could hear everything that went on in the cubicles if you were close enough, even though you tried to convince yourself that no one could hear you when you were the one trying not to be heard. But those partitions were pointless—just fuzzy, wobbly dividers to tack vacation pictures onto so you could look at them and think about being someplace else while you were sitting at work with no intention of doing anything that didn't have to get done right away.

Andrew was talking on the phone, just work-talking, that voice he put on when he was being Office Guy. I hated that voice. He used it that last time, when he was pulling on his thin black socks and keeping his back to me. *We've come to a stopping point,* he'd said. We've come to a stopping point? What the hell was that? As if I hadn't just licked that area behind his earlobe, just how he liked, as if I didn't even know that was the way he liked it. I didn't sit up, just stayed under the pink-and-white striped sheet, staring at his thick back, at the way it sloped forward at the shoulders. I wanted to kick him off the bed. I should have. He was practically but not completely divorced from his wife, and he had a kid, a little boy in kinder-garten, and it made me sick when I thought about that part of it so I tried not to think about it. About that boy, hugging his dad, after he gets home from working all day and then sleeping with me, and those pudgy little-boy hands on his dad's back, patting him, feeling safe now that he's home. Does a mom tell her son his parents are practically divorced? Or does she wait to tell him on the day that dad doesn't come home from work? I didn't want to think about that part.

So I deliberately walked past the opening of Andrew's cube, slowly and sort of swishing my hips with each step, and I figured I'd wait another hour and then try to listen again.

The breakroom was filled with paper: paper cups, paper coffee filters, flyers on three bulletin boards trying to sell TVs or SUVs or old computers, reams of copier paper stacked in the corner, rolls of brown paper towels lined along the back of the counter. It smelled like paper in there—still and rough and dry. Like my hands, the way the cheap soap in the breakroom left them, and then I had to dry them off with that rolled brown paper, exactly like grocery store paper bags. I kept two bottles of lotion in my cubicle, one for dry skin, one that smelled like magnolias.

For almost two months, Andrew and I used to meet in the breakroom at 10:15 and 3:15 every day. It was the most perfect time we spent together, sweet and teasing, brushing hands and hips, not able to say anything but *How's your day?* and *That phone won't stop ringing* and *Is it five o'clock yet?*—which, of course, meant: *Can we have sex soon, because I can't wait any longer.* When we finally did have sex, it was rushed and intense and usually partially clothed, and I always got messy and wet and wrinkled, and then he left quickly so he could go home and hug his son. We always did it at my apartment, because I live two blocks from the office, and then after I always stayed under the sheet and listened to him close my front door and waited for the sun to go down all the way outside my bedroom window, and then I'd heat up a frozen dinner and scroll through my phone until I was tired enough to sleep. Or sometimes I'd order pizza and watch a movie, which was usually on the better days, the ones when he stayed in me a little longer and said things like *Jesus god you're so hot,* which I didn't quite believe, but sometimes, with my tongue on his neck, it did feel possible.

It wasn't that I wanted anything real with Andrew. Not really. If he officially left his wife, and we officially became a couple, everything would change, and things like meeting in the breakroom wouldn't feel as good. But there's nothing good about being left, left without reason or even excuse, and I thought it would be nice if Andrew's life hurt for a little while. So at 2:20 I went back over to his cube, stayed just outside the tall partition, and fiddled with my watch and my three rings and my fingernails and hoped I wasn't so obvious that someone would mention it to Andrew later. Mary Ellen probably would eventually, but hopefully by then I'd have some dirt on him, some satisfaction in knowing that he's particularly miserable right now.

"Bunch of assholes," he was saying, and I knew I was getting the good stuff. "If they don't want me here, fine. I've got so much shit on Pryce. He won't know what hit him." Then something about the Astros. I didn't even know he watched baseball. Then, "It starts tomorrow." And then he was quieter, and I couldn't make out the words, so I put my rings back on the right fingers and headed for Mary Ellen's cube.

"Something's going to happen tomorrow," I said, nodding my head toward Andrew's cube.

"Oooh. What?" She rolled forward in her chair.

"Don't know. But keep your eyes open." I wasn't a gossip. I wasn't even social, avoided talking when I could. But Mary Ellen brought out that side of me sometimes, with the way she made me feel part of something secret and interesting.

The next morning I spent forty-five minutes blow-drying my hair with a round brush, so it would be fluffy and reflect the fluorescent lights, like Andrew noticed the first time he talked to me about something besides work. I wore my highest heels and my soft blue A-line skirt, and I thought about Andrew's hands on my thighs, and then thought that it didn't really matter if the hands were Andrew's, but that it was just nice to have hands on my thighs.

I got to work at twenty to eight, early on purpose so I didn't miss anything. Only three people were there so far, and Andrew's cubicle was empty. I walked past it a few times, then peeked in one time, and then stepped into the cube and looked at the pictures on his desk. His wife was fat, not super-fat, but surely her thighs were not the kind Andrew liked to touch. His little boy was kind of fat too—in that way that hinted at a bigger fatness to come. Andrew wasn't fat, but his body was solid. I felt little when he was on top of me.

The phone rang and I yelped and left the cube. I walked by Pryce's office. The light was off, the door was closed. I wondered what Andrew was planning to do. For a minute I felt jealous that he had a plan to do something. Then I went to my cube and turned on the computer and did little back-and-forth swings in my chair.

The eleventh time Andrew followed me home from work, he hadn't started kissing me right away after I closed the door. He just leaned into me so I was pressed up against the wall, and he looked at me for what seemed like a long time. Probably two minutes, which isn't that long but definitely seems like it when someone is just looking at you, that close to you. Then he slid his hand up the front of my sweater, just one hand, and pulled one breast out of my bra and just held it, looking right at my face the whole time. Then he started the regular kissing stuff and I don't remember much else about that time. But the beginning, that part comes back to me at the strangest times. Like in line at the cafeteria, I'll suddenly feel like his eyes are on me, like his hand's pressed into my breast, and I'll just lose it for a minute. Short of breath, the whole thing. Crazy.

At 10:15 I walked by Andrew's cube on the way to the breakroom and he still hadn't shown up. That made me so angry. I mean really. I'd gotten to work early and everything. Mary Ellen walked past me, looked back over her shoulder with that knowing sort of look she has. When Mary Ellen went into the breakroom, I turned around to walk back to my cube. Pryce was in his office with the door half-open, and his assistant Jenna was out in front on the phone like she usually was. I stood at the side of her desk and waited for her to hang up. She kept glancing over at me, annoyed, but finally hung up.

"Hey Lacey," she said. "What can I do for you?" She started flipping through the datebook on her desk.

"Is Mr. Pryce busy?" I asked. "I mean, could I meet with him for a minute today?"

"Regarding?" she asked without looking up.

"A personal matter," I said, not even sure what I'd say to him if I had the chance.

"1:00," she said.

"Fine," I said.

When people started clearing out for lunch, I went back inside Andrew's cube, started rummaging around to find something, some kind of proof to offer Pryce so I wouldn't come off like a complete idiot. And there were those damn pictures again. One was Andrew and his wife on a beach, tacked to the cube wall, and they looked sunburned and happy. Then I went through his middle desk drawer and under the inkpad was a square of fresh white paper, with my name written on it twice—Lacey Lacey—one right under the other, and then a small, lopsided heart at the end like a period. That heart got to me. It was like something a grade school girl would do, and I loved that, and it made me want to die. I put the paper back under the inkpad, closed the drawer, went back to my cube. Sat in my chair and swung back and forth. Took out a notepad and tried to draw that heart, one side fatter than the other, the bottom point crossing like a tiny X. But I couldn't quite get it. It didn't look the same.

At 1:00, I stepped inside Pryce's office, trying to decide what to say. I'd never actually been inside Pryce's office before, just seen slices of it from the half-open door when I'd walk past it on the way to the breakroom. The wood in the office, on the desk and the chairs and the little table against the wall, was dark reddish-brown, and had a shine like it had just been polished. The lamp on the table was too delicate to go with all that dark wood. Its thin shade was like silk, a mint green with beaded trim. Maybe the wife bought it for him. Or more likely, Jenna did, Miss Executive Assistant, the one who did everything for him, dial his phone for him, empty his trash can. The lamp wasn't turned on, and when I looked down I saw that it wasn't even plugged in. The cord was draped along the floor, no outlet in sight. Just for show, that lamp, and Pryce wanted it right there, even though he couldn't plug it in.

When Pryce asked me to sit down, I jumped forward too quickly. Deep breaths, I thought. The chair in front of Pryce's desk had a rounded back, burgundy leather with copper studs all along the top. I sat down, rested my hands on the studded arms for a minute, then folded them in my lap. Pryce picked up his phone and started talking to Jenna, even though her desk was right outside his office door. His voice was loud and occasionally cracked, and she could have heard him fine without the phone.

I looked around while Pryce talked, focusing on the row of pictures along the wall. Pryce with some big-wig, then Pryce with a couple big-wigs, then Pryce playing golf with a different big-wig. Pryce's face looked the same in every picture: squinting, lips pressed together into an almost-smile, his cheeks full and red. His hair always had the same gray sheen, lacquered down, not moving.

"Dammit," said Pryce, banging down the phone. "Damn girl." He stomped past me, yelled, "Take a break, Jenna," shut the office door, then stomped back to his chair. He leaned back, so far back in the chair that I thought he might topple over. "Well," he said, looking at me for the first time. Then he looked at me too long, too hard. "Lacey Drake. Accounts."

"Yes," I said.

"You wanted to see me." He leaned forward, still looking at me, taking me in, trying to figure out what I was doing in his office. Deciding what to do with me.

"Yes. I wanted to see you." What the hell was I doing in here?

Pryce's mouth formed a smile that didn't seem to belong on his face. He stood up, walked around the desk, keeping his eyes on me. Leaned back against the desk, right in front of me. "You've worked here awhile now, haven't you?"

"Almost two years," I said. It was hard to look at him. I looked at my hands.

"So." He crossed one leg in front of the other, and now his shin was resting against my knee. "What is it that I can do for you?"

As I tried to think of something to say, trying not to think too hard about his leg against my knee, it occurred to me that maybe Andrew's big show-the-boss-who's-boss thing could be just not showing up for work today. Maybe he thinks that not doing anything can feel like something, something important, a decision that matters. That made sense to me, which I hated. I hated that I was sitting in this office now, with the smell of it all around me—a heavy mix, like expensive cologne and cheap furniture polish. I hated that I'd spent my day waiting for Andrew to show up. That I'd ever waited for him. Or for something that felt like him.

Pryce leaned down, closer to my face. "What does Lacey Drake from Accounts need from me?" He pressed his lips together into that almost-smile, and his leg pushed its way between my knees, quietly, casually.

The strangest part was that along with feeling startled and repulsed and angry, I felt strong. I felt like I could slide forward in this tall leather chair, keeping my knees tight around his thick leg. I could drop my head back and look up at him and have whatever I wanted, at least for today. I could convince him that Andrew was going behind his back, stealing from the company, something. I could leave work early with Pryce, spend the afternoon sweaty and moist and messy. But I knew the smell of this office would hang on me all day. I knew it would tighten in my stomach later, at night, alone in bed with nothing better to think about.

I stood up, which was not a great idea because then I was so close to him, his thigh against mine, his face looking right down on me. I made myself look at him as I spoke. "I just wanted, I wanted to say, I have to leave."

"You don't have to leave," he said, his breath hot on my face.

Pryce and Andrew got tangled up in my mind, heat and guilt and power, and every bit of my skin was prickling like little heartbeats, and I had to choose something. Right away, before I didn't do anything, and it all just happened to me again, and I let it, and I learned to like it.

"I'm leaving. I have to leave." I stepped to the side, moved away from him. "I, because, I found another job."

His face was red and round, and I turned and went to the door, walked out of his office, straight to my cubicle. I turned off my computer and grabbed my purse. I stopped at Andrew's cube and stole the little square of paper from his desk drawer, his Lacey Lacey with the heart. I walked past the breakroom, left the building, went to my car.

The afternoon spread out in front of me like a gift.

Three Days of Rain

Nothing like rain she said and he laughed and they ran fingers along necks and thighs for everafter days, nothing but *this*, rain falling like splinters, digging in. Until he cupped her face in one open palm, said *Sunny today*, words dropping down like solid things. Like his footsteps. *No*, her legs did not want pants, her feet could not bear the roughness of the floor. He left for not-her. She cleaned her kitchen. Windows-open sunnybreeze clean. Days passed. She mowed the lawn into patterns, opened mail with a knife. Each moment felt like dry echoes of his lower lip, her bare legs, hot tea morning air. She remembered how normal days felt. Eating upon rising. Sleeping through the night. The absence remained, a hole she'd climb into, an open hand along sidewalks, a curve in her bed. She said *Nothing but this*.

Volcanic Glass

Fred

Yesterday I hit a stunning young woman with my car. It was the most truly awful moment of my life—not a statement I would make lightly, as there has certainly been some competition in my 43 years for that particular distinction. In fact, it seems every day holds some bit of awfulness for me, like this morning when I walked right into the mailman. I wasn't paying attention; it was completely my fault. His bag fell and a handful of letters scattered along the sidewalk. I wanted to apologize, or help him pick up the letters, but I couldn't bring myself to look at him, and besides, nothing seemed appropriate after ruining his morning like that. So I coughed and looked away and hurried to my car.

Of course, as I drove to work this morning, all I could think of was that young woman. She's fine, luckily, a slight concussion I was told, and it seems all fault has been placed on her chemically altered state. I didn't know about the drugs until later, though, and when I found out I was perhaps more disturbed than relieved. My first glimpse of her as she appeared in front of me, right in the middle of the road, was all limbs and hair, endless hair, whipping and twisting as she fell. When I got out of my car, saw the languid beauty of her body bent into a sort of dancer's pose beneath the front bumper, the feeling of dread was so thick in my chest that I couldn't swallow. Her eyes were open; I had been shocked to see her eyes, alert, brilliant really, looking up at me with no trace of emotion. Her face was thin, too thin, with cheekbones too harsh to rest beneath those eyes, but her simple beauty staggered me and I smoothed my hair and tried to flatten the unironed pocket of my shirt. The back of my neck was stinging and hot. I couldn't speak; I just looked at her delicate face, waiting for the police to arrive, hoping someone had called them.

I suppose I knew it then, as I looked at her, but it wasn't until this afternoon that I finally made the decision. It was time for me to go to the volcanoes. I've been wanting to study the Hawaiian arc of volcanoes since I was eleven. That was the year I had to get glasses, thick glasses, heavy enough to never quite stay on straight, and as I wore them I sat low in my desk at the back of Miss Pittipski's sixth grade classroom. I eventually discovered an intense comfort in the natural disaster books that lined the back wall, protecting my face from unwanted attention by looking down at the glossy pictures of the Hawaiian arc. I memorized those pictures, felt the draw of the volcanoes in their neat line, waiting to erupt. It didn't happen often, the eruption, but I knew I wanted to be there someday when it did. Later, in high school, I started to check out books from the library and found I was also intrigued by the mythology, by stories inspired by the volcanoes. Virgin sacrifices flung into volcanoes to preserve the natural order. Death to maintain life, bones and flesh and hair consumed by molten lava to nourish the earth. The lava, even trapped in those pages, looked like liquid fire, incandescent, living and breathing. I wanted to see it up close.

I've filled out four grant applications in the last two years, fully intending to go to Hawaii and do field research on the volcanoes, but the applications never seemed to find their way to the mailbox. The time was never quite right. There was always a reason to stay in Ohio, to keep my stable job teaching geology to high school sophomores, students who were 15 and 16 and weren't new anymore but still felt they had forever to go until graduation, teenagers who simply couldn't care less about the types of feldspar or the viscosity of magma. I had been warned by my mother, over and over, that I would regret teaching high school.

"Fred, honey, those kids'll eat you alive," Mom would say, or some variation of that sentiment. I knew what she meant, and her intentions were good. I suppose I'm just not particularly fond of dealing with people, and I do tend to avoid the meaningless conversation that acquaintances, and even strangers, seem to insist on. But it's different when I'm teaching the kids, somehow; everything falls into place, makes sense. I don't mind grading their quizzes, writing "You rock!" and "Gneiss job!" at the top. And I don't mind the lectures, like today, talking about the principle of dynamic equilibrium. I've said those words, written them across the chalkboard, for almost twenty years now, but it always feels a little new somehow.

"Dynamic equilibrium," I said slowly, drawing out the syllables as I scratched them across the board. I turned and grinned at my students. "Exciting, yes?" A low murmur of laughter answered me. "What is it, what is it? Ryan?" Ryan unfolded himself from his desktop and looked up at me, his heavy brown eyes almost awake.

"Mr. Clark, I don't think that was in our reading last night."

"Oh, Ryan, nice try. But no such luck." I waited out the snickers before turning back to the board. "Okay. Dynamic equilibrium." I underlined the words. "Interconnectedness!" I began writing the definition as I spoke. "The state of interconnectedness among the earth's major components. And what are those components? Hailey?"

"Oh. The major components. That would be, like, the components of the Earth?"

"Thank you, Hailey, for that lovely clarification. Yes, the major components of the Earth. The atmosphere, the geosphere, the hydrosphere, and the biosphere. Right, Hailey?"

"Right, Mr. Clark," she said, rolling her eyes, smirking.

"And these components, my friends, exist in a state of changing balance. They impact each other! A significant change in any one of them will result in a change in all the others. Yes?"

"Yes," echoed my students lazily, humoring me, scribbling my words in their notebooks. I appreciated their efforts, slight though they were, but I was no longer sure they were enough for me. The students weren't interested, would never find any excitement in the things I loved, like earth and air and lava and rock, the things that continually build up and break down around us. And, of course, hitting that woman yesterday had to be a sign. My car, a good car, the kind with power everything, had been like a reminder to myself, why I was still here, how rewarding it could be to have a secure job with a steady income. But now, sitting in that car, all I could see was the accident, and that woman's eyes, and the sleepy, blank faces of my students. And the volcanoes were calling. So it was time to go.

Melanie

"When the car hit me, it started to rain." That's what I remembered, and that's what I told him. I didn't mention the part about tasting the rain, soft, salty, letting it melt like candy on my tongue. Or how the raindrops, splatting against the ground and the car and my face, sounded like firecrackers, the kind I got to play with when I was a little girl, those long, crackling strips. I didn't say how they told me later it wasn't raining.

"Oh," he said, quietly, not looking at me. "So, that's all you remember?"

"Mostly," I said, then laughed. I could also remember looking up at him after he hit me, how he just stood there and stared at me and fidgeted and turned all red in the face. But the one thing I definitely couldn't remember was what I had done with my shoes, which really bothered me because they were my soft black flat shoes with little strings at the toe that made me feel like a ballerina, like I was floating above the ground. I liked floating. I laughed again, louder this time. I wasn't trying to be mean, but really, what did this strange little man want from me? Why was he here? He hit me with his car, and yes, I was too high and walking down the middle of the road with no shoes on and it was my own fault, but that didn't give him the right to show up here, in rehab hell, this white and shiny place with its eyebrow-scrunching people who pick me apart daily. I hate this place. Everyone here walks carefully, them and us, as if the ground were splintered, and the voices are always hushed while they relate and express and the other meaningless things they keep asking me to do.

"Well, I just," he paused, took off his giant glasses and breathed on them, wiped them with his shirt. "I felt awful. I kept thinking that I should have done something, or said something."

"It's okay, don't sweat it." I touched his hand, but he jerked away from me like it hurt. "It wasn't your fault. I told the cop that, too. They couldn't really charge you for hitting me anyway. I was flying high in the middle of the street. I guess unless I had died or something." I stopped when his face went white. "But I didn't, right? Just a concussion, just stuck in this lousy place." I touched his hand again. I couldn't resist, he was so jumpy and everything. It was funny, almost sweet. His back straightened and he coughed, one of those fake polite coughs, pulling his hand away to cover his mouth.

"So, I should be going," he said, "but I'm glad you're okay." He stood up too quickly and bumped his knee on the table. I didn't laugh this time. He started to leave but then turned back to me and said, "I wanted to give you something." He handed me a little folded cloth, soft like snow, and I unwrapped it because I figured that's what you do when somebody gives you a present. Inside was a rock. An actual rock, flat and deep black and shiny. We weren't supposed to have personal items in this place, but I took it out of the cloth and curled my fingers around it, holding it like a secret. I didn't know what to say, what you're supposed to say when the guy who hit you with his car gave you a rock. So I just looked up at him and smiled.

"It's obsidian," he said to me, all eager and beaming. "Volcanic glass. It's formed by lava cooling beneath the surface of the earth." He picked up the cloth and folded it. "It's something I've been carrying around for a while now. It has, I guess, helped me through things. Sort of like a promise that things will get better. Maybe it can be that for you." He looked at me, into my eyes, for just a second, then tucked the cloth back into his pocket.

"Hey, thanks," I said. He turned away then, sort of smiling and sad, leaving me with his little volcano rock.

I tried to describe him later to Ray, but I couldn't think up the right words. It didn't matter, though, because Ray just understands me. He's the only person in this place who can. Ray's easy to talk to because he's not a user. He's an alcoholic. Drinking just seems more romantic to me, more forgivable. I can never talk to other users. They go on and on about the white hot rush and the clarity and they don't listen, just give you all their bullshit insights on life, trying to prove how deep they are. I don't get it, don't need to hear it. It's not like that for me. It's always been like air, a way to breathe. I didn't start with pot as a kid and graduate to coke and get sucked into crack, the way so many describe it here, and excuse it. I just met a guy at a club and he knew exactly how to kiss, consuming, slow and soft and melting, and back at his place he smoked a rock and offered it to me like it was a gift, like his lips. After a couple months he didn't want me anymore, but I still wanted his gift. The high was hot dancing bodies and soft-soft lips melting onto mine. It kept the blood in my veins from stopping. It, this thing, this drug, was in me, it was part of me now, and I accepted that and held onto it tightly.

I said all of that to Ray, too, and he listened to me, really listened, made me feel like my words were important. That's why last night I gave him the rock, the volcano rock I mean, from the guy who hit me. Ray was leaving in the morning, and he was all worried about going home to his son, saying he was a rotten dad and how could his son ever respect him or forgive him. I don't know anything about kids, but Ray's eyes blinked fast and his chin shook a little when he talked about his son, so I felt like I should do something. The rock was all I had to give him. I didn't need it anyway. I'm not going to change, not going to get helped through anything. This is who I am, frozen, waiting for those lips to come to me again.

Ben

The day my dad came home from rehab was the same day my guidance counselor called me into his stuffy brown office at school. I didn't even know I had a guidance counselor. But at least it got me out of gym class, flag football. I hate gym. So I went in there, nervous I guess. I thought maybe the school found out about Dad, and this counselor was going to preach to me about forgiveness or whatever. I didn't need to forgive Dad. I never blamed him or anything. He works all night, sometimes two shifts in a row. It sucks. Maybe I'd be drinking too, if I were him. Who knows. But I didn't want some stranger telling me that. It was mine to know, not his to give me. Not in that ugly brown room. It didn't matter anyway because it turned out there was just a problem with my schedule for next semester. When I left the office there were still twenty minutes left in gym class, and I was supposed to go back, but I decided to walk really slow through the hallway and count floor tiles instead. That was sort of like exercise.

When I got home that afternoon, Dad was already there, sitting in his plaid reclining chair like he'd never left it, waiting for me.

"Hey, Dad," I said. I didn't really look at him, but I could tell he was looking at me. I couldn't remember him ever looking at me much before, so I sat on the couch across from him.

"Ben, hi. Son. I'm back, I'm home."

I still didn't look at him because it was kind of weird how he called me son. "Yeah, that's great, Dad," I said.

"I just want you to know that I'm not drinking, not ever again. I'm home now. We're going to be okay. We're going to be really good."

"Okay," I said, finally looking at him. I didn't want to tell him, but he sounded more drunk now that he did before.

"I'll never wind up in a place like that again," he said. "But some good came out of it. That's what matters. And Ben, I met this lady while I was there. Melanie."

Oh, great. I didn't want to hear about some affair or something. That's all I need, my parents get divorced, joint custody, weekend visits. "Oh," I said.

"Melanie gave me something the night before she—well, she took a whole lot of pills. They weren't even sure how she got them." Dad looked at me kind of sideways, uncomfortable, like he wasn't sure if he should keep talking.

"Oh yeah?" I tried to keep looking at him.

"She had the saddest face I've ever seen. And hair, so much hair. She would talk to me for hours, never making much sense, but I just listened because she seemed to need it. Although it must not have done much good." He made a sound, almost like a hiccup. Then he stretched back in his chair and pulled something out of his pocket. "She gave me this." He held up a black rock, kind of turning it so the light glinted off it.

"A rock?" I asked. It didn't look like a real rock, like in the dirt. It was totally smooth.

"Yes, well, she said it's supposed to help you, make your life better, something like that." He handed the rock to me. "I don't know how true that is, but I want you to have it. It'll be like a reminder, my promise to you. I want to make things better for you, Ben." Dad stood up then and I could tell he'd lost weight. That made me sad and I wasn't sure why.

"Thanks, Dad," I said. I closed my hand around the rock and hugged Dad with my free arm, then went upstairs. I slept really well that night. I didn't dream at all.

Yesterday, instead of going to gym class, I went to Mr. Clark's room, the geology lab. It was his free period, the secretary said. She didn't know if he'd be in there or not, but I figured it was worth missing gym to find out. And he was there, sitting at his desk, holding a piece of paper in one hand and an envelope in the other. He was staring off at nothing, or maybe he was really seeing something, I don't know, but he looked weird. I started to back out the door but he turned to me then, squinted at me through his crooked glasses, and I figured I should say something.

"Mr. Clark? I'm Ben, and I need more credits for next semester, and the office said your class was full, but if maybe I talked to you and got a signature on this form it might be okay if I took it." I set the form on his desk, cleared my throat, and waited for him to move or at least breathe loud or something. He looked like he couldn't believe I was really there in front of him.

"You want to study geology?" he asked me. "Why is that?"

I pulled Dad's rock out of my pocket and showed it to him. "My dad gave me this, it's about the only thing he ever gave me, really, and I looked it up and it's called obsidian. Volcanoes make it." I looked at Mr. Clark, and his eyes were wide, looking at the rock, but he didn't say anything. So I kept going. "I thought that seemed pretty crazy, how something dangerous could make something beautiful like this. It's strong but, like, quiet or something." I stopped, feeling stupid, but then Mr. Clark pushed his glasses up on his nose and looked straight at me, like I was saying something important.

"Yes, it is beautiful, isn't it?"

"Yeah," I said. "Sort of amazing that this cool thing can form while it's just sitting there, letting the lava pass right over it. So I was just reading about all that, and I thought maybe geology wouldn't be such a bad class to take. You know, if you have room for me."

He paused for a second, and I thought he might say no. I went all cold and my stomach felt strange. The rock was slick in my hand, and I watched how it reflected the yellow class-room light. Obsidian, I thought. It was a good word. Finally,

Mr. Clark stood up. "Of course," he said. He signed the form, Frederick T. Clark, Geology, and handed it back to me. Then he picked up the paper and envelope he'd been looking at and threw them in the trash can by his desk. "Ben, it will be a pleasure to have you in my class." He looked down at the rock in my hand, then back up at me. "See you next semester."

What We Remind Ourselves to See

Impossible to know the worlds alive inside another. That man behind the counter who won't say the total amount due, waits for me to read the numbers on the register screen. Simmering with anger. He hates this work, hates that he must work, after years upon years of giving himself up to an office, to a hardened boss, to only be let go. Let go, like a falling, like release. Let go without pension, without benefits. And so he is here, angry at me for ordering food from him, for giving him money that is not his, that goes into the drawer in its ordered slots. He goes home to a wife who sleeps in most days. She asks him to bring home dinner on his way. She is old and tired. She is glad he still works.

The woman who honked and swerved and scared my children. Sped off with such rage. She defines her life as tragedy, and she can, it is. She lost her mother to cancer, lost her innocence too young, too violently. Her latest boyfriend was kind for a while before finding release through a slap, hard, open-palmed.

This man in my house, even him. I know who he was when we first met, who he has become in these years with me.

But so many layers are left unpeeled. Hopes that he still clings to, and the ones he has let go. Let go, like a falling, like release. Anger at the menial work he must do, at the lack of so much, at me. And love, love for things I do not even know he loves. He wants to live on a boat, catch lobster, wear a thick fisherman's sweater on a beach by a campfire, preparing his dinner over flames. He wants the waves to rush at him, the sound to fill him, the water to wash everything rough away.

Minor Spasms

Ed was tired of thinking about her. It happened at the most inconvenient times, in the shower, driving his car, lying in bed trying to fall asleep. It was hard enough falling asleep, with his bad back. He didn't need his mind replaying the most painful parts, the hateful things she said, the way he sat there and took it. He wanted to turn it all off, wished for an off switch to shut out the memories. It had been a long month. He was tired.

The scene his mind replayed the most was the final one. He had a last chance without knowing it, and he blew it.

"I'm leaving you."

"You always say that, Maybelle."

"Well this time's for real."

"You been saying that for years, plum. You're not going anywhere."

"Well, that's exactly right. You finally got it right. I been going nowhere my whole life with you."

"May. Plum."

"Don't call me that. I'm done being food for you. You're weak with me, I don't know how the hell you'll get on without me. But I'm sick of wondering. I'm leaving."

The house was quiet without her. Forty-six years of her voice filling the rooms was a hard thing to suddenly be without.

He kept the TV on a lot. That helped quiet her voice some-times, the things he knew she would've said that echoed in his mind and throbbed through his back.

He rolled out of bed and looked at the Polaroids taped to his wall. Grandkids mostly, but here and there a picture of Maybelle. She didn't smile much, had that kind of face that looked stern even when she was perfectly happy. But he loved her. She was his wife. He never thought she'd really leave. He ran his finger over a shot of May holding their first granddaughter. His wall of pictures was the only part of this house that was really his. May decorated everything else. Every upholstered chair, every ivory lace curtain; it was all her. He couldn't figure out why she'd want to leave this place, her place. You'd think she'd kick him out before she'd go herself. But she did hate his pictures.

"Jesus, Ed," she said one day. "How tacky. Put them in an album like a normal person, for Christ's sake."

He never did take down the pictures. He needed some-thing in this house that was his.

"They're on my side of the bed, dammit. Just don't look at them."

Sometimes he had to change the tape when it got too yel-lowed, but he never took any of his Polaroids down. Just kept adding more. The grandkids had always loved his camera, back when they were young. He would take pictures of the kids, maybe dressed up in Maybelle's hats, or standing next to each other to see how tall they'd grown, and then he'd give them the black shiny square with the white border to hold. They'd hold it delicately, by the edges like he taught them. Blow on it, he'd say. Just lightly, now. The kids studied the pictures carefully as they developed, watched the colors begin to form out of the black, the images gradually taking shape. He let them keep the ones they liked, and he'd tape the rest to his wall. Then the kids would snap his camera shut—it was the kind that collapsed, the kind they didn't even make anymore. The new film still worked in it, though, so he didn't see any reason to buy a new camera. He'd just slide the camera under the table next to his bed, ready to use at the next visit. Maybelle had never used his camera. She used her phone to take pictures, just like the kids did now.

A house filled with kids made him happy. He never expected to be alone like this. Without Maybelle around, each day was taking a long time to get through. Maybe she was right. He was weak. She was the strong one, and now he was alone and he was weak. Maybelle had always done the bills, bought the food, tidied up. He just worked at the candy factory and brought home the money. Now that he was retired, he didn't even have that. He felt like he might just blow away.

You need to get off your duff and do something with your life. He could hear her saying the words clearly in his head.

"Maybelle, my life's about done for. Now's when I get to enjoy life, not worry about doing something with it." He spoke out loud, even though she was no longer around to hear him. She was still there, in a way. She was in the white-on-white sitting room with the navy blue accents. She was in the fish-themed bathroom. Powder room, she called it. He could still feel her everywhere.

Damn lazy fool.

The refrigerator was about empty, so he decided he'd better get some groceries today. Maybe some of those microwave TV dinners. And some soda, some real soda, not that diet stuff May always bought. He got dressed slowly.

What are you, color blind? Put on a different shirt with those pants.

"Why do you care what I look like?" he said to the empty room. "You never look much anyway."

Not much to look at.

He drove to the grocery store with the radio on, drowning out the sound of her voice in his head. He wheeled his cart around the store for an hour.

There's the peanut butter, Ed, right there in front of you.

"How the hell are you supposed to find anything in here? Everything's out of order. It doesn't make sense. Why can't they put the damn peanut butter next to the bread?"

A young man in a maroon apron came over to him. "Can I help you, sir?"

"Oh, no, son. I'm doing just fine. Don't you worry about me."

He thinks you're crazy, talking to yourself like that.

"Well, if you'd just leave me alone, I'd be fine."

You said you didn't like it quiet.

"I changed my mind."

"Excuse me?" A woman with a baby on her hip was looking at him.

"Not you, Miss. I wasn't talking to you."

"Oh, sorry." She pulled her baby closer and walked away.

She thinks you're crazy, too.

"Well, you made me that way."

He finally pulled into the check-out line. His cart was pretty full by now. Ten TV dinners, a few cans of soup, bread, peanut butter, jelly, milk, a case of soda, a box of vanilla wafer cookies, a bag of pretzels, and some bulk candy in case the grandkids stopped by. They were getting older now, of course; they didn't come around much anymore. But better to be prepared. He used to bring home candy from work every Friday and fill up one of Maybelle's jelly jars with Mary Janes and taffy squares and little root beer barrels. His own kids and his grandkids had all liked the candy dots the best. Chalky pink and yellow and blue dots, stuck to those long strips of paper. They held the paper up to their mouths for minutes at a time, biting the dots from the paper, stopping only occasionally to chew. He couldn't get dots too often from work; they were a big seller and the boss had been stingy with them. But when he did bring them home, the kids went right for them. He sighed; he hadn't talked to his kids much lately, not since Maybelle. Didn't want to admit it to them, or to himself. But here he was, alone at the grocery store. Couldn't deny that.

The young lady in line behind him didn't have a cart. She was just holding one of those awful tabloid newspapers. She had long blonde hair, straight as a board, like Maybelle had when she was younger. He and May had been sweethearts since they were in the tenth grade together at St. Catherine's. That hair was the first thing he noticed, caught his eye right away, long and swinging. Jennifer, their oldest girl, had blonde hair until she was three. Then it started getting darker, like his own. He cleared his throat. "Miss, I've got quite a load here. You can go in front of me if you'd like."

Wow, such manners. I thought you forgot how to be a gentleman.

"Well thanks, Pops. You're all right." She moved past him and set the paper on the checkout counter.

Ha! Pops.

"Shut up."

"What the hell did you say?" The girl turned around sharply and spit the words at him.

He felt his chest constrict. "Nothing," he said quietly. "I wasn't talking to you, Miss. I'm sorry."

"Well then who the hell were you talking to, grandpa? Your invisible friend? Huh? Your dead wife?" She laughed, a wheezing sort of laugh that rang through his ears.

"She's not dead," he said, his voice barely a whisper.

Weak. You're old and weak.

As the girl walked away, he noticed her backpack was half-zipped, over-full.

That little hooligan. Shoplifting at the grocery store. I told you, Ed, time and time again I've told you. This neighborhood's going to the dogs.

He paid for his groceries with cash, since he wasn't quite sure where Maybelle put the checkbook. Kept meaning to look for that. He didn't turn on the radio as he drove home. He started remembering all of Maybelle's complaints about their neighborhood.

You just wait and see. Before long, it won't even be safe to live here anymore.

He hadn't thought much about the comments at the time. He just chalked them up to more whining, her need to always complain about something or other.

Our kids used to play in that alley, you know. Kicked the ball back there. It was safe. Now, nothing but bums and broken bottles. Right outside our back door.

That must be why she left, he decided. The real reason. It was the neighborhood. Maybe she thought he wouldn't be willing to move. It made sense to him now. He picked up the phone as soon as he got home.

"Jennifer, hi sweetie, it's Dad. Have you heard from your mother?"

"Dad, thank god. She's upstairs. I wanted to call you, I almost did a couple times, but Mom kept asking me not to. Listen, Dad, she cannot move in here. Tom's been having a fit. Can't you two make up?"

"Of course we can, sweet pea. I'm gonna clear this all up. Get her on the phone."

"Great. Hold on."

He started putting things in the refrigerator as he waited. Milk, TV dinners. Should the soda go in the fridge? Maybelle kept it on the back steps. But he liked it cold.

"Hello, Ed."

"May. Sugarplum. Come on home now. I figured it out." He cradled the phone with his shoulder and bent down to put the soda on the back steps.

"What did you figure out?"

"I know what's been eating you. I just didn't see it before."

"I thought I made things pretty clear, Ed."

"I'm sorry, plum. You know it takes me a little longer than it should sometimes. But look. If you want to move, we'll move. I'll take you out of this neighborhood. We'll get ourselves a house somewhere real pretty." He leaned against the refrigerator door and sighed deeply. It would be good to have her back. Whining and all. He missed having her around.

"Oh, Ed."

"So what do you say?"

"Ed, it's not that easy."

"What're you talking about, May? Come on home, we'll call one of those real estate guys, we'll get ourselves a new place. Easy as pie."

"I'm not running away from the neighborhood, Ed. I'm running away from you."

He sat down at the kitchen table. "Now, May," he said softly.

"You know better than this, Ed. You know it's not about the neighborhood. Stop fooling yourself. You need to accept that I'm not coming back."

He sighed.

"Ed, I've got some good years left in me. I want them to be mine. Yes, I'm being selfish. But that's what I need to be right now."

"Plum." He rubbed his hand across his forehead.

"I don't want to live with you anymore, Ed. And no, Jennifer," she said, raising her voice. "I'm not staying here either. I'm going to get a nice little apartment all my own."

"Good grief, May. We have this big house, with all your fancy decorating. Why would you want to go live in some apartment?"

"Ed, I'm going to hang up now. I'm sorry it has to be like this. You'll get along okay. I'm sure you'll find a way to manage. The kids will be here for you."

"No. Maybelle, don't go." He listened to the dial tone for a few minutes before hanging up. Then he sat at the table for almost an hour, hearing the sounds bounce around his head, her words, the low buzz of the refrigerator, the rasp of his own breath. When he finally stood, he felt a sharp pain in his back, the lower left side where it always hurt the worst.

"At your age, you can expect some minor spasms," the doctor had said. The pains didn't feel minor to him. Maybelle used to tell him to plug in the heating pad and stop moaning about it. But when the pains started up, nothing really seemed to help. He took two pills anyway, muscle relaxers, and washed them down with a warm soda.

He made his way to the bedroom. "I'll just take a nap," he said out loud.

Lazy.

"I'm not lazy. I'm in pain."

You don't know pain, Mister. Let me tell you about pain.

He fell asleep with Maybelle's words pulsing through his lower back, achingly, relentlessly.

The room was completely dark when he woke. He had heard something. He looked at the clock. Almost one in the morning. Guess I needed that nap, he thought. Then he heard it again. A clinking sound, like something hitting a window. He swung his legs over the side of the bed, then slowly raised the top half of his body. He knew to be careful after back spasms. They could start right up again if you moved the wrong way.

Then came the crash. The sound of glass breaking. He froze.

I told you. Didn't I tell you? Gone to the dogs.

He should call 911. No phone in his room. He should have a phone in his room. He should get one of those new fancy phones like May.

Glad I got out when I did. The strong survive, Ed. You might as well give in right now.

I'm strong, he thought.

You're weak.

"I can be strong," he said quietly. He heard more noises, scuffling, glass falling to the floor.

Weak. Can't even get off the bed.

He stood up and walked toward the hall. He just needed to get to the phone.

I don't want to live with you anymore.

He stopped when he heard muffled voices. More than one person. In his kitchen.

I'm sorry it has to be like this.

He wouldn't make it to the phone without them hearing him. He stepped back toward his bedroom. He could just hide. Maybe they'd just take the TV and leave.

That's it, Ed. Hide.

He stayed close to the wall as he walked back into his room. His hands felt the pictures taped up by his side of the bed.

Tacky.

"Be quiet, Maybelle," he whispered.

He reached down beneath the bedside table and pulled out his Polaroid camera. He popped it open, straightened his back, and walked out into the hall.

More sounds from the kitchen. Laughter, maybe? The voices sounded young. He kept walking.

"Grab the soda too."

Definitely a young voice. He inhaled deeply, then stepped into the kitchen. He took a picture.

"What the hell?"

He took another picture. The flash bit through the dim room.

"Get your knife out, man."

Another picture. Each one slid to the floor as the next one popped out.

"Man, he's taking our picture."

"Let's go, Danny."

"Shut up, Nick. Just tell the world my name why don't you."

Flash.

"We're out of here."

He watched through the lens as the boys climbed back out the window. When they were gone, he flipped on the light. The pictures were in a pile at his feet, the colors slowly appearing and taking shape.

One of the soda cans had exploded as it fell down the back steps. He ran the water until it was hot, wet a rag, and mopped up the mess. His back was feeling better, from the pills, he supposed, and the nap. Even bent over, cleaning, he felt okay. He picked up the case of soda and put it inside the refrigerator. He found the broom in the hall closet and swept up the pieces of glass. Have to get out the yellow pages tomorrow, he thought, and call someone about that window. The pictures were still on the floor, fully developed now. He took them back to his room.

The house was quiet as he taped the pictures to his wall. He stretched out on the bed, closed his eyes, and listened to the silence.

Quarter to Four

Restless, I step from your bed in that place between night and morning, wrap myself in your coat, walk the dark air with its dusky streetlamp glow that enters me with a terrible joy, like lies I tell the moon. We once walked, you and I. Oceans turned over, you tripped on a bent stick, stopped, offered it to me like an answer. Our feet kept time. Past beaches of shells and salt, past pyramids and tombs, past ourselves. Now dandelions whisper away each step, white-posted rows of mailboxes curl this court. Cool licks of breeze find my skin. A corner of sun breaks open the sky like an egg and I remember myself. I count the things that must be done.

Color and Noise

Claudia was almost entirely certain, in the way only someone who has carefully weighed and considered every facet of a situation can be almost entirely certain, that she should break up with her fiancé. She stood outside Trevor's apartment door as she contemplated this thought. She pressed the doorbell again. Claudia wore a pale linen dress, pearly lipstick, high-heeled sandals. Her skin smelled of berries and flowers. Her fingers were bare. Trevor was not her fiancé.

"Okay, Mom, you can look now." Claudia opened her eyes. She watched as her daughter Mandy swirled dramatically, her skirt an overwhelming cloud of tulle and lace and white-white pearls.

Mandy paused for effect. "What do you think?"

"So beautiful, sweetie," Claudia said, trying to sound motherly, trying to forget the girl she once was, standing on Trevor's doorstep. She had married Frank, they'd had Mandy, and now Mandy was getting married. This was her life.

Mandy turned back to the mirror and her gown followed a second later, crinkling and swooshing into place. "So this is the one." There was a tight, pleased crook to her smile.

Too much poof, really, Claudia thought. But this was Mandy's wedding; she was the one who had to feel pretty, look confident. Claudia's opinion wasn't important. "It's perfect, Mandy."

"Definitely. Daddy'll love it." Mandy lifted her mass of dark, ironed-straight hair, reaching beneath to undo the line of tiny clasps. Mandy looked just like Frank, was every bit her Daddy's daughter. Pale skin, light enough to see the hint of veins across the hands, the feet; hair so deep brown it was almost black; the shock of blue eyes, so disturbingly bright that they hurt to look at for too long. Both Frank and Mandy were thin and willowy, with limbs that went on and on. Claudia was nowhere to be seen in her daughter. She was short, com- pact, and basically one color from head to toe: beige. Beige skin, beige hair. Frank called it honey-blonde. Claudia called it beige.

Mandy couldn't quite get the gown undone. "Let me help," Claudia said. Her fingers were hot against the cool skin of Mandy's neck, and Claudia pulled back slightly. She wasn't entirely familiar with how it felt to be this close to her daughter, even though they still lived in the same house, with Mandy staying there to save money before the wedding. Mandy kept to herself. She rarely let Claudia glimpse more of her world than was necessary.

Once the layers of skirt were completely stepped out of and hung up and smoothed down, Claudia cleared her throat quietly. "Mandy. Before you do this, I just want you to be sure, I mean, this is a big step." Claudia glanced down, studied a smudge on her plain white tennis shoes, then looked again at her daughter. Mandy seemed too thin, her long, bare feet curled against the cold dressing room floor, her striped panties stark against her colorless skin. "You're, you know, sure about this, right?"

"Mom, of course. The dress is perfect."

"I just, not so much the dress, but you and Aaron. I just wondered if everything, getting married, if it was all going okay." Claudia softly bit her tongue to stop the words. They didn't sound the way she wanted them to.

"Everything's fine, Mother," Mandy said harshly. Her eyes were empty now as they looked at Claudia, without a trace of their earlier bride-to-be, diamond-reflecting gleam. "But fine. If you don't want the dress, we won't get the dress." Mandy pulled on her jeans and black sweater and walked out of the dressing room.

"Don't be angry," called Claudia from behind the curtain, her voice straining to be heard. Claudia was almost getting used to her daughter's theatrics. Mandy was taking college classes, majoring in Communications, but really only wanted to act. She went from show to show in her community theater group, preparing her audition for the next play before the current one's final performance. There had been a period of about six weeks when Mandy spoke exclusively in a British accent. She often corrected Claudia's pronunciation of words like "git" and "warsh," saying that she had learned in her Voice and Articulation class how truly Midwestern this sounded, how embarrassing.

Claudia tried, without much success, to be less embarrassing for her daughter, to limit her words when she spoke. But even Claudia's written words offended Mandy. Claudia had a degree in journalism, but she paid the bills by writing movie review blurbs for the local paper. Mandy never went to movies. She thought they were frivolous entertainment, beneath a trained stage actress like herself; she resented being even loosely connected with them through her mother. Mandy always sighed deeply when she walked past Claudia and her laptop, or pointedly coughed over the click-click-clack. Claudia would never admit it to Mandy, but she loved her job. She loved the movies, even the bad ones, with all their color and noise, their movement and life. And it always amazed Claudia how easily the words came when they were spilling onto a page, how much better she sounded on paper than in person.

Eventually the saleswoman peeked her head into the dressing room, and Claudia said, "Sorry, she, well, we've decided to wait." She walked out to her car where Mandy was standing, arms folded across her chest, eyes anywhere but on her mother. Claudia handed her the keys.

While Mandy drove them home, Claudia closed her eyes and heard Trevor's doorbell in the back of her mind. She heard the creaking of floorboards and the doorknob turning and his voice on her skin, the stale cigarette breath brushing across her perfumed ear. Felt Trevor's fingers slide her dress from her shoulders, watched it fall to the floor. She heard her laughter ringing through the musty hallway.

That night, Claudia and Frank discussed Mandy. Their discussions were always about Mandy, or Mandy's life, or their lives as they related to Mandy. At least these talks were a break from the painful quiet of their daily lives together. Claudia often thought, in the hush of evening, as she watched her husband read his weekly golf magazine, feet up, glasses slipping down his nose, that she was gradually being swallowed up by silence.

Claudia was trying to control her voice. "Well surely it meant something or she wouldn't have done it."

"Claudia, honey," Frank said gently.

"Just stormed right out of there."

"She's just nervous, Claudia. Of course she wants to get married. You're reading too much into it." Gently, gently.

Frank rested his hand on her shoulder. Claudia flinched at his touch, but it seemed that Frank chose not to notice such things. His touch was respectful, too respectful, almost reverent. He was safety and comfort, everything soft and smooth and real. He held Claudia quietly in his arms, looked closely at each line creasing her forty-something face, then held her closer still. As he always did. His tenderness ate at her slowly.

Claudia had tried to break up with Frank three times during their long dating period. The others Claudia had dated, the ones she so wanted to keep, eventually grew tired of her, got distracted by other things, other girls. Except Frank. He never let her go. Claudia appreciated this and resented it with equal force. Frank wore his kindness, his forgiveness, like a shiny merit badge. He always held her after sex. He always called it making love. She had known it would be sensible to marry him, was sure he would always treat her well, never leave her. He would be a good father. He was a good man. She reminded herself of this daily.

"Don't get worked up about all this," he said. "Mandy's fine."

"Just forget it," Claudia said under her breath, mostly. She unwrapped herself from Frank's arms and smiled thinly at him. "Forget I even brought it up. I'll take care of it myself."

Claudia didn't exactly intend to follow her daughter that Friday night. If it hadn't been for the phone call, the male-but-not-Aaron's voice asking for Mandy; if Mandy hadn't hurried out the door, her face flushed, just as Claudia happened to realize they were almost out of milk, and that she should probably just run to the store while she was thinking of it; if the rainy dusk hadn't hidden her nondescript gray four-door so well, and made it so simple to follow at a discreet distance behind Mandy's puttering car, then she wouldn't have done it.

Claudia followed Mandy, feeling like she was in a scene from the movies she reviewed. As her daughter parked near a row of apartments, Claudia turned off the headlights. She kept the motor running as she watched from across the street, several buildings down. A young man ran through the rain to meet Mandy at her car, hugged her close and long, kept his arm around her as they ran back inside together. Claudia couldn't breathe. She noticed vaguely when the rain stopped. There was a violent aching in her chest, a specific pain that recalled others like it: Trevor saying goodbye; Claudia saying I do. She forced air into her lungs, then exhaled loudly, a raspy sound that startled her. She turned on the radio, found a noisy song she had never heard before, and drove off with a speed that shook the steering wheel beneath her damp hands. As she drove, she tried to slow her breath. She needed to think straight, to help her daughter make the right choice, to do what Claudia couldn't.

Mandy's fiancé Aaron lived in the green house on fraternity row by the university, and Claudia knew that on a Friday night, a mother would not be a welcome sight at a frat house. She knew her pleated slacks looked ridiculous as she climbed the crumbling concrete steps and knocked on the door, several times, waiting to be heard above the music and laughter and hollered conversations. She knew she should give up. She tried the bell.

A girl in a clingy orange shirt finally opened the door and shouted, "Yeah?"

"Aaron. I'm looking for Aaron, Aaron Chase. Do you know him?" Claudia's hands were now tight fists, and her fingernails pressed sharply into her palms.

The girl laughed and turned away, but called "Aaron!" into the thumping room in a loud, squeaky voice. She turned back to Claudia and said, "I think he went out back when it stopped raining. Go down the steps and through the gate." She laughed and squeaked and closed the door.

Claudia found Aaron stretched out in a reclining lawn chair under the back porch awning, a beer bottle in one hand and a cigarette in the other, wearing only baggy boxers and a choker necklace of shells. He looked up at her, surprise barely registering on his face, and said, "Hey, Mrs. Peters."

His stomach was flat and strong and Claudia found herself squatting low on the porch next to his chair. "Aaron. Hi, Aaron." She moved her eyes away from his stomach. "Aaron, do you know where Mandy is tonight?"

"Oh, sure, Mrs. Peters. She's got play practice." He smiled at her, his teeth bright even in the dimness of the night, his lips wet with beer.

"That's what she told you?" Claudia knew Mandy was consumed by theater, took it seriously enough to rehearse on a Friday night, maybe even seriously enough to leave her fiancé alone at a party without a shirt on. But Claudia had seen it, had seen them. She saw their arms around each other in the rain.

"Yep," said Aaron. He sucked in deeply on his cigarette. "Why, what's up?"

"I saw her, Aaron. I saw her with someone." Claudia wanted him to move, to react, but he just looked at her steadily. Her breathing quickened. "She hugged him. They went into his apartment." Her voice was getting louder. She was almost shouting now. "I think you should call off the wedding. Call off the wedding. You have to call it off."

Claudia realized she was crying, hot tears, heavy as they slid down her face. She stood up but did not wipe her cheeks, did not look away from Aaron.

"Mrs. Peters, don't worry. I'm sure you got it wrong." He was sitting up now, his long legs straddling the chair. "Why don't you go on home now, and talk to her when she gets back? Okay, Mrs. Peters?"

He was humoring her, she felt it, and she took a step backwards. "Just think about it, Aaron. Tell me you'll think about it."

"Sure. I'll think about it. And don't you worry, okay? Everything's fine." Aaron leaned back again, crossed his bare feet at the ankles, brought the beer bottle to his lips. A few girls draped along the porch railing snickered. Claudia turned away, trembling, her heels sinking into the wet grass as she walked back to her car.

No one was home. Mandy was still out. Frank always spent Friday nights with the guys from work, which Claudia pretended to resent. She didn't want to think yet. She walked straight to the bathroom, filled the tub with too-hot water and foamy bubbles. She took off her clothes quickly and slid in, eyes closed, mind closed, sinking deeper into the water, finding comfort in the heat and the crackling bubbles. It wasn't Trevor she thought of, not his musty apartment, his rumpled bed. It wasn't Aaron, not his tight skin, the skin his daughter's lips must taste often. She saw, instead, her own face, the way it must have looked to Trevor, lifted and happy and open; she saw the lips he kissed, sometimes for hours, the mouth that smiled, sang, laughed, moaned for him. She saw the Claudia that Trevor saw.

Claudia stayed in the water until it was almost cool, until her toes and fingers were puckered, until she heard the front door open. When no voice announced itself, Claudia knew it was Mandy returning and not Frank. She blotted her skin hurriedly and wrapped herself in the towel.

"Mandy?"

"It's me," she called out on her way upstairs.

Claudia stopped at the bottom step, one hand on the rail, the other holding her towel together. "Where were you, Mandy?"

"Rehearsing." She turned to go.

"Where?"

"With my friend James."

"Your friend."

"We're doing a scene together for Acting II." Mandy sat down on the top step, one leg tucked under her. "He had this amazing breakthrough with the blocking." Her face was brighter than usual, her voice more high-pitched, but none of the emotion was directed toward Claudia. Mandy was just performing. "He's keeping his back to the audience the whole first half of the scene, sometimes even blocking me from view. It's brilliant. It changes everything." This last bit was said almost accusingly, as if Claudia had somehow prevented this dramatic revelation from taking place sooner. Then Mandy paused, staring at her mother, until Claudia felt uncomfortable and looked away. "Mother, do you really need to walk around the house like that?"

Claudia saw that her towel had slipped too low in front. "Sorry," she said instinctively, then wanted to bite back her words, to drip messily in front of Mandy without remorse. Still, she pulled the towel up higher and wrapped her arms around her chest.

"I'm home," called Frank. He locked the door before walking toward them.

"Hi, Daddy." Mandy smiled at him with a warmth that Claudia never felt, not in this house, not as this Claudia.

"What are my girls up to?" He looked at Mandy as he spoke.

Claudia couldn't decide if she believed Mandy or not. She was beginning to see that it didn't matter. It wasn't Mandy who needed help; Mandy's life wasn't the problem. Claudia's life was the problem.

Frank kissed Claudia lightly on the forehead, then stepped back. "Honey, what're you doing out here in a towel? You should put some clothes on."

Frank's words made Claudia want to laugh, full and hard, to make the air shake and the walls quiver, to make something stir within her husband—something tangible that Claudia could grab onto with both hands. But Frank was just looking at her, just her face, no lower, with a sort of quiet confusion in his painfully blue eyes. *Put some clothes on.* Claudia didn't need to laugh. She needed to leave, finally, for good. To leave Frank and Mandy and the stillness of this house. To walk out the door in a burst of color, with music swelling and the credits rolling behind her.

"Aaron's calling," said Mandy, digging in her purse for her cell. "I have to take this." She headed toward her room.

"Mandy, wait." Claudia thought her voice sounded strong now, almost felt she could step up on top of it. She looked at Frank, then back at her daughter. She was done with this marriage, done with this role. Mandy would be married and on her own; Frank would be fine. Time for her exit. Claudia uncrossed her arms and let her towel drop to the floor.

#9 LaPuerta Drive

Last year, or was it yesterday, I drove past your house and remembered how much I miss the morning paper, damp and unrolled, with hot milky black tea and sugar cubes. I forgot how much I love the perfect flat sides of sugar cubes, how they plink in the mug and fade down. You set one on my tongue, remember that? It took so long to melt, so sweet, I forgot how sweet. And that pink rise of sun, the clouds scraped through the light. My stomach fell just seeing it. Once we watched a thunderstorm, every inch of sky lit by flashes of white, almost too white to see, too fast. Standing on the porch in the wind, rain hitting down like blades, like firecrackers, handfuls of them. I forgot how much I love storms. That umbrella you gave me, remember? With the painting on it, the painting with umbrellas, men holding them, in tall hats and long coats. I never knew how much I'd miss that umbrella.

Places to Hide

The Treehouse

Meg sat in the backyard, cross-legged on the crumbling patio, with the summer heat spun around her like cotton candy. Her little-girl arms were slippery with coconut sunscreen. She picked at weeds and moss in cracks of concrete, watching the sprinkler wave back and forth, so she could pretend she wasn't watching her father.

He was teasing her mom, pulling the bikini strap from her shoulder. Then he untied the back, ripped it off, laughed as she crossed her arms over her bare chest, as she ran into the storage shed to hide, its rusted doors squeaking, scraping together.

When he draped the flimsy top outside the door, just in his wife's reach, her hand peeked through to grab it. She covered herself again but didn't leave the shed, waited for her husband to lose interest and head back toward the house.

He caught Meg's eye, said nothing. Meg looked away and walked across the damp grass to the back fence, to the treehouse.

Her father built the treehouse. It was remarkable, a child's dream. A good place to hide. With three floors, it reached as high as the tree was tall, and extended all the way below to the earth. At the bottom was the dungeon, cave-like and cool, an area of dirt and rocks encircled by thick roots. Billowy petal fragrances were trapped there, from the lilac tree with its dripping lavender clusters, from the giant bush with its feathery pink flowers that blossomed into white pom-pons as big as grapefruits.

The second floor of the treehouse could be reached through a trap door in the dungeon's roof or by climbing long blocks of wood nailed to the outside trunk of the tree. Boards surrounded this second level: wooden walls with open slats to peek through, a sturdy bench with a back rest, and a makeshift ladder stained deep brown that reached up through a hole in the ceiling, like an attic.

On the third floor, at the top of the treehouse, the air smelled like rain. Breeze slid easily through branches and leaves, whipped hair around sunburnt faces. The half-walls sloped outward on all four sides, making the top floor feel open and free, even dangerous.

Later that afternoon, Meg looked up from inside the dungeon to see her father climbing the treehouse. She hugged her knees to her chest, uneasy, resenting this intrusion into her hiding place. She watched as her father hung a tire swing from a large branch. He used a full-size car tire, powdery with black dirt, attached to a heavy, braided rope. Meg didn't leave the dungeon until he was done.

"Will it hold me?" she asked her father. "Is it safe?"

"Of course," he said. "I built it."

But she worried that she'd swing too high, that she'd fall.

Home Movies

"Turn and smile," Meg's father said to her and her brother, pointing his soundless movie camera at them as they climbed the treehouse. He had them wear nice clothes for the camera—for Meg's brother, a shirt that buttoned, with the long, pointed collar of the seventies; for Meg, a linen dress, shoes that buckled, socks with lace. "Laugh," he said, scripting their enjoyment of his treehouse, his creation. "Wave. Wave to me."

His camera captured scenes that would never occur without his direction. In the fall, he told his wife to film him as he raked leaves into piles, then feigned agony, wiping imagined sweat from his forehead, staring at the pile, his hard-earned job well done. When the family watched the home movies later, this was funny. Meg laughed at her father's exaggerated expressions, his pretend emotions. She liked watching herself and her brother leap into the movie's frame, squealing with the silent laughter of old films, hitting the pile feet first—remembering the crunch, the scent—watching the dulled colors as leaves flew up and back down around them. Inside those images, the world felt happy and safe. But mostly the movies focused on her father and the elaborate scenes he created for himself.

Meg wanted to blame her father for the way her life turned out. For the waves of sadness she felt, the anxiety, the pain that didn't seem to have a cause. She thought it would be easier to blame him if he'd done something really horrible. Like how her friend Callie once told her about the night her new stepdad pulled her onto his lap, said how pretty her breasts looked, how grown-up, and asked politely if he could touch them. Callie mentioned this so casually it made Meg's stomach ache for days. But Meg's father never did anything like that, nothing too bad, too obvious. Just small things that stayed with her, like the time he looked at her and squinted his eyes and said she should use more conditioner on her hair. Or when she was little, the way he'd pull her knuckles to hear them crack, laughing as she squirmed and cried out for her mom. How he reminded her, like he was doing her a favor, that shorts made her legs look heavy. Then after the divorce, his frequent, dramatic phone calls canceling his every-other-Sunday visits. Talk and talk and talk of dreams, all his own.

Office

After Meg and her brother finished high school, their father moved from the Midwest to Florida. He gave them a speech first, explaining he was leaving, saying he needed more sun in his life. Now and then, sometimes on birthdays, they'd get a card signed *Dad*.

Meg tried college for a little while, then a different college, then a community college, always dropping more classes than she'd finish. She worked as a waitress and hated it and quit. Then worked in an office and hated it and stayed. Fluorescent lights flickered and buzzed overhead, keyboards pattered, phones rang. The company was small and old-fashioned, filled with silver-haired, well-dressed men who smoked cigars and took long lunches. Meg's boss reminded her of her father—his hair slicked with a bit of wave in front; the stoutness, the stocky arms and legs; the wide face that smirked rather than smiled. And this: the dress code set by her boss required his female employees to wear skirts and heels. When someone finally complained to Human Resources, he amended his requirements: female employees may wear pants, but not with socks, only nylons.

He relied on Meg, his personal secretary, to get him through each day.

"Can you fax this, pronto?"

"Of course." Smiling.

"Honey, would you type this up A.S.A.P.?"

"Right away." Ignoring the *honey*.

"I can't find my glasses."

"Here they are." Again.

She made coffee that she didn't drink. She filed letters she didn't write. She had tiny, stinging cuts on her fingers, but she filed quickly, accurately. She made her boss happy. Meg was not happy. She knew this job was another way for her to hide. Her days were tightly scheduled, busy, pointless.

Stage

For a while, Megan fancied herself an actress. Frustrated with her days at the office, she looked to her nights for diversion. Theater suited her, put her in a comfortable state: wearing a costume, following a script, giddy with the fun of make-believe. She knew her enjoyment of performing was probably something she got from her father, which gnawed at her a bit, but she loved it anyway. She loved rehearsals, pretending to be someone else. She loved dating actors. She loved the moment before the play began—peeking through the curtain to see how many seats were filled, listening to the audience as they would leaf through the playbill, comment on the theater's strange beauty, wait to be entertained. Their noises were hushed and reverent. Behind the curtain, energy was flying, stomachs turning. Meg did vocal warm-ups and ran through her lines, rolled her shoulders, stretched her neck. She powdered her face and got into costume, hid inside the character she was about to play. She was Susannah and made strangers laugh; she was Laura and made strangers cry. Theater was like therapy, like candy, like living.

Marriage

After dating men who were always canceling dates—who said things like, "You're wearing *that?* "—Meg met someone who asked her to marry him, a man who was calm and kind and nothing like her father. She did not invite her father to the wedding, did not even consider it. Ten years passed without seeing him, without missing him. Meg settled into a life of comfort, in a home that felt safe. She spent evenings curled up on a soft gray couch with her husband. She ignored phone calls, let them go to voicemail. It was a good way to hide.

Her father still called now and then, left messages, saying things like, "I want to know you again." Meg would listen to his voice, clearly older, recognizing bits of it—its heavy pauses, the drama of his words, the practiced sorrow. She'd wait for the click as he hung up.

Her husband would squeeze her hand, knowing she didn't want to talk about it. But those calls always stayed with Meg. She'd wonder how her father could still make her feel like hiding, why she couldn't delete the old messages, block his number. Feel like she was standing at the top of that treehouse, free.

Fractured Girl

Above my fireplace hangs a chalk and pastel drawing: a fractured girl, fragments of her delicate frame scattered across the canvas. A triangle in a top corner holds only her fingers curled around her toes. A square section at the bottom bares a shoulder, rounded, hiding a lowered face. The colors are deep, strong—emerald green, ocean blue, scarlet red. My husband drew the picture years ago when he was a student. He is an artist; he doesn't see just a girl in this picture. He sees the messiness of life, how broken we all are. I am a mother; I see a girl. I ache for her, long to scoop up the lost pieces of her, to put her back together. Maybe that's because as a mother of sons, I don't have a little girl of my own to take care of. But mostly, when I look at this girl, I see my sister.

Long before I ever gave birth, I played mother to my sister Emily. She already had a mother, our mother, but I was four years older, felt wiser and better and more important. I didn't treat Emily like a sister, or as I imagined sisters should be, like sisters on old television shows who brushed each other's hair and talked about their boyfriends. I lectured her about how she should pluck her eyebrows. I scolded her when I caught her smoking a cigarette or skipping school. My only connection with Emily was showing her all the ways she wasn't good enough, wasn't enough like me. Throughout her high school years, as Emily's life got messier, I offered pointless advice, thinking she needed as many overprotective mothers as she could get: *Drugs, bad. Running away, bad. Taking a shower, eating breakfast, keeping a job, good.* When Emily turned twenty-one, I tried to stop lecturing, just stood back and watched as she continued to use drugs and deny herself food, empty her mind and disappear into other people. Emily wanted desperately to be liked; she became whatever her current friends wanted her to be. She had many friends when they needed her, and none when she needed them. As I saw what Emily's world was really like, I wanted to close my eyes.

Emily would go for days without sleeping. She'd stay up all night covering her bedroom floor with pages of scribbled notes and drawings, maps to the confusion of her mind. Her heightened emotions led to irrational, and even violent, behavior. She'd write countless bad checks; when her boyfriend hit her, she'd hit back harder. Emily would drop out of sight for a while with no explanation, then suddenly reappear, smiling, ready to pick up where she'd left off. Eventually, when she'd wind down from her high—sometimes high on life, sometimes high on drugs, usually both—she became sullen, withdrawn, hollowed-out. She stopped looking me in the eye. She became Depressed Emily.

When Emily was diagnosed as manic-depressive at twenty-two, she was put on medication that seemed to numb her. Her movements were heavy and careful. Time slowed while she lifted an arm or raised her head. She crossed a room as if she were sleepwalking. She didn't stay on those drugs long, preferring instead to turn back to drugs of the non-prescribed variety, the kind that increased her thirst for life instead of quenching it. She could have chosen to try different medication, to find one that would balance out her moods, her life. That was not what she wanted.

It was Manic Emily who called after I hadn't heard from her in almost two years. Emily was now twenty-five; I was twenty-nine, married, and a mother of a one-year-old. The phone rang at two o'clock in the morning.

"Hey, sis," she said, her voice too chipper, too loud. "I'm pregnant. Very. I need help, okay?"

Emily always needed help, and I knew I'd never really given her the kind of help she wanted. I hadn't missed her during the past two years, didn't think enough about where she might be, what she might be doing, if she was all right. I hadn't acted like her sister, and I certainly hadn't felt like a mother to her anymore. Our mother was worried sick about Emily. I wondered why Emily had called me instead of her. I shook my husband's arm and whispered, "I have to leave. An Emily crisis." I peeked into my son's crib and kissed his forehead before I left.

I drove to the 24-hour copy shop where Emily had used the phone. My fingers tightened on the steering wheel when I saw her leaning against a light post. She looked wasted away, sunken and empty. She looked dirty. Skin clung to the bones in her cheeks; her hands seemed too big for her arms. Her belly bulged outward without being round, without seeming to carry life. I thought of the *National Geographic* magazines that used to pile up at our grandma's house, those naked brown boys with their thin limbs and swollen stomachs, eyes like glass.

"Hey," she said as she climbed into the car. "You care if I smoke?"

I pressed the button to lower Emily's window. She knew what I was thinking; I didn't have to say it. I wasn't her mother.

We went to an all-night donut shop and sat at a cold metal table for an hour. Emily never touched her coffee. She talked about her boyfriend Vic ("The cops took him in again, but just for reckless driving and no license, so they probably can't hold him too long"); she talked about the friend who'd kicked them out of his basement where they'd been staying ("That asshole, we told him we'd figure out how to get the money"); and finally she found her way to the reason she wanted to see me. Vic didn't want any part of "all that blood and crap" at the hospital when Emily gave birth, and Emily didn't want to go through it on her own.

"So I thought maybe you'd be my labor coach."

Emily was being induced in four days. She had never gone to a prenatal class, never read any books about childbirth. She needed to be taken care of. But I didn't want to do it.

"Vic should be there," I said. "And what about Mom? Don't you think she'd want to be your coach? Have you even told her you're pregnant?"

"She knows. She wants me to live with her. She acts like I'm twelve. I can't deal with her right now." Emily lit another cigarette. "Besides, you have a kid now, right? You've done this before." When she tucked her hair behind her ear, I saw a crude tattoo, probably home-made, on the side of her neck: *Property of Vic.*

I had met Vic only once before, when Emily's car broke down a few years ago and they needed a ride. But once was enough. From the power he seemed to hold over my sister—convincing her to hand over her paychecks to him, or quit jobs to spend time with him, or shoplift for him—I had expected him to be imposing, even frightening. He was small. Shorter than Emily, younger than her, bonier. His mouth hung slightly open, showing dim spaces where teeth should be. His hair was long and greasy; his face was long and greasy. His few words, spoken only to Emily, were coarse, unkind. He never looked directly at me.

"New tattoo?" I asked. "Is that Vic's artwork?"

"You don't understand." Emily put out her cigarette, flattened her palms against the cool tabletop. Not once since I'd picked her up had she rested a hand on her stomach. Not once had she curled her arm under that bulge, felt for a kick, paid any attention to this addition to her body at all. I remembered the first moment I learned I was pregnant, how natural it felt to immediately cup my hand around some imaginary swell. I looked at Emily and wanted to say, *Touch your stomach*. Instead, I studied a crease of skin along her neck, right across the center, a dingy, crooked line of indented flesh. When I gave my son his baths, I'd struggle to hold him still long enough to scrub those creases. If I missed one, the dirt would keep collecting. Better to catch it right away, or later I'd have to scrub so hard it would hurt.

"Emily, do you want to be a mother?" I asked. "Are you keeping this baby?"

She didn't seem surprised by the question. "I don't know."

"Adoption?"

"I don't know." Emily's face was completely shut down now. Her hand was at her lips, her fingers shaking. She needed another cigarette. She needed much more than that. "Well," she said, "will you be my labor coach or not?"

I'm not sure why I said yes. I suppose it was for her, at least partly; for the baby, hopefully; but probably, I said it for me. To our mother, I was the Good Daughter. This was my role and I played it well. When Emily messed up, she made me look better. I felt better about myself. I used her to put my own life in perspective: I might be deep in credit card debt, but at least I wasn't living out of a car, like Emily. Now she was pregnant—okay, so I would rub her shoulders, tell her to breathe. I would calm her between each contraction and let her squeeze my hand through the pain. I'd play mother again.

The day before Emily was induced, Vic called her, told her he was sorry. Emily said they had talked all night. As I drove her to the hospital, she spoke nonstop about him. Vic promised he'd cut down on the drugs, swore he would never yell at her again, and insisted that she keep the baby. I wanted to lecture Emily, tell her Vic was not someone who wanted to take care of a baby; he couldn't take care of himself. He just wanted what was his—as Emily was his, his personal branded property.

When we arrived at the hospital, I helped Emily fill out the forms for uninsured patients. Then we were directed to a room with no windows, a room used to store supplies. Metal shelves reached to the ceiling, bursting with cloth and paper and rolled sterile gauze. A mechanical bed was tucked in the corner. The lights were too bright. The walls shook and buzzed from some sort of construction going on in the next room. During labor, nurses came in and out without knocking, restocking other rooms, taking little notice of the almost-mother inside. I brushed my sister's hair. I painted her toenails. I tried to pretend everything was perfectly normal. But I knew what my own labor had been like: a picture window, a padded rocking chair, a husband rubbing my back.

Five hours later, right before delivery, Vic showed up. They fought immediately; evidently, Emily had admitted to a nurse that she'd done drugs that morning. I stayed close to the wall as Vic shouted at Emily for saying too much. Emily shouted back, pleaded, begged. The nurses finally came in as Vic grabbed Emily's arm. They told him he was being disruptive and he'd have to leave.

"That's bullshit," he said. "It's my damn kid."

The nurses tried again, saying only one person was allowed in the room with Emily during the delivery. He should go.

Emily said, "My sister can wait out in the hall."

The doctor made eye contact with me and shook her head: *Stay*. Vic stood at Emily's side; I moved to the end of the bed by her knees.

When it was time to push, Emily kicked, and I had to hold her legs. She cursed harshly at me, the doctor, the baby— everyone except Vic. I was angry at her for this embarrassing scene, for the way she didn't seem embarrassed at all, and for everything she'd done to get herself to this point. I was humiliated by how the nurses looked at me, how they assumed I was everything that Emily was. I wanted to shout, *I'm the good one!*—except this wasn't about me, and it certainly wasn't about Vic. It was only partially about Emily. As the doctor finally delivered the baby, as the amniotic fluid splashed across my shoe (with Emily saying to Vic, "Did that crap get on you, babe?"—her reaction to the moment her daughter was born), it was clear that right now, only this baby mattered.

Then I knew something was wrong. When I gave birth to my son, as soon as he had been delivered, the doctor put him in my arms. Emily's baby girl was whisked away to a table set up in the corner. Her skin was purple. She didn't cry. My son had wailed from the instant he hit the light.

Two nurses rubbed the baby vigorously, her delicate arms, her curled-up legs, the length of her thin back. They rolled her limbs between their hands like they were kneading dough, willing it to rise.

I looked at Emily, but she was looking at Vic, not her baby. Before I could stop it, before I could scream it away, I had the thought: *If the baby dies, she'll be safe.*

At last, as the baby's skin faded to a more human shade, the noises began. There was no sudden shriek, no moment when everything became okay. There was only a resigned, hiccupping cry, a giving-in to this desire for her to breathe.

A nurse asked, "Do you plan to keep the baby?"

My sister asked, "Can I have a cigarette?"

When I went home that night, my husband and I brought our son to bed with us. We curled him into our blankets, rested our fingers on his belly, his toes.

It was not until five months later that Emily officially gave up her daughter for adoption. Soon after birth, the baby had been placed in a foster home; Emily was allowed supervised visitation rights until she could prove she was drug-free and had a secure home and steady employment. She tried for a while. She went to work, went to counseling, even went to church. Then she stopped.

The day the adoption papers were signed, I got a call from Depressed Emily. I took her to lunch; I listened to her sadness about the baby, and her fears that Vic—who had left in anger the day before—would never stop blaming her, would never return. We both knew, though, that he'd be back. He always came back. When Emily's fries were gone, she asked, "You think I can crash at your place for a while?"

I could have done it. I could have taken her in, given her food and a bed, babied her. But I had my own baby at home now. Emily had decided not to be a mother, and I didn't want to be a mother for her anymore.

She laughed at my hesitation before answering. "Come on, sis, just for a couple days." She smiled at me.

"No," I said.

It was the last word between us that meant anything. After that I could only say things like "Where can I drop you off?" and "Bye, Emily" and "Take care," as if care were a thing she could take with her, to use when she needed it.

How To Dance

This desert hangs down like stone around you. Pretend you don't long for moon-soaked fields to stretch your limbs against those cool blades. Let heavy sun skip through you. Each wrinkle forgets its place until, after the sweat and sigh of day, night cracks apart with echoes like smoke on your tongue. Blow the dust from your lips, wet them with whatever nectar finds you. Let this desert sand burn and bleach your feet. Step as if the earth has no pull.

Acknowledgments

"Sketching Venice"—Honorable Mention, Micro-Fiction Contest, *River Styx*

"The Former Mrs. Jonathan Rothdale"—a version won the Jim Haba Poetry Award and appeared in *Mid Rivers Review*

"Worse than Wanting"—appeared in *Untamed Ink*

"Things that Break Us Right Open"—appeared in *Mid Rivers Review*

"The Train"—published online by *Fiction Weekly*

"Daylight Savings"—a version published online by *A Story in 100 Words*

"All is Well"—a version appeared in *Organic*

"When the Rain Stops"—published online by *Foliate Oak*

"Mothers"—appeared in *Adelaide Literary Journal*

"Devoured"—a version appeared in *Cuivre River VI*

"Volcanic Glass"—a version appeared in *Adelaide Literary Award 2018 Anthology*

"Color and Noise"—a version appeared in *Organic*

About the author

Beth Mead received her MFA in Creative Writing from the University of Missouri-St. Louis. She feels lucky to have studied with writers Mary Troy, David Carkeet, Lex Williford, and Catherine Rankovic, and grateful to now pass on their wisdom to her own students. Beth is a Professor of Writing and Director of the MFA in Writing program at Lindenwood University in St. Charles, Missouri. She is the editor of *The Lindenwood Review* literary journal. Beth developed Lindenwood's graduate writing program to include a fully online option, along with the on-campus coursework available, and expanded the MFA curriculum to include a wide variety of writing genres and focus areas for writers. Along with workshops, craft classes, and literature classes in fiction, poetry, and creative nonfiction, Lindenwood students can study scriptwriting, narrative journalism, literary journal editing, the publishing process, the novel, and genre fiction, including young adult, romance writing, and science fiction. Focus areas are continually added for intensive study of specific authors, books, and writing styles. Students can attend the MFA Craft Talks series, student/alumni readings, and other literary events hosted by Lindenwood. More information is available at www.lindenwood.edu/MFAwriting. Beth lives in O'Fallon, Missouri, with her husband, Chris, and her sons, Connor and Casey. Her fiction, poetry, and creative nonfiction work has appeared in journals such as *Adelaide Literary Magazine, Fiction Weekly, Cuivre River VI, Mid Rivers Review, Noise Medium, Untamed Ink*, and elsewhere. She won the Jim Haba Poetry Award and was an Honorable Mention in the River Styx Micro-Fiction Contest. Her story collection *Dancing Madly* explores how we keep trying to survive in our flawed ways as life breaks us down, sends us spinning—that mad dance that gets us through each day.

www.ingramcontent.com/pod-product-compliance
Lightning Source LLC
Chambersburg PA
CBHW020025030726
47499CB00007B/2273